D1525627

The Mother-in-Law

Judy Moore

ISBN 13: 978-1976080609
ISBN 10: 1976080606

Excerpt from *The Mother-in-Law*

Victoria stepped out onto the patio, ambled around the pool, and stood at the gate, gazing out at the moonlit beach and listening to the waves crash against the shore. She inhaled the moist sea air and basked in the soft touch of the salty air against her skin.

The cool ocean air felt refreshing until she realized goose bumps had begun to appear on her arms and then across her entire body. Something was off, and it was giving her chills. She had a feeling that she wasn't alone. A sixth sense told her that someone was watching her. Her body tensed, and she squinted out into the darkness.

Scanning the patio, she slowly turned around toward the house. Then she saw her, saw her silhouette, standing in the window staring down at her. Her mother-in-law didn't move away from the window, didn't wave, but just stood and stared down at Victoria. Victoria held her gaze for what seemed like at least a minute. Then, finally, the drape slid across the window, and her mother-in-law was gone.

To all the wonderful mothers-in-law in

the world—who are nothing like this one

Acknowledgments

Thank you so much for the support, feedback, and encouragement in the writing of this book to Eunice Moore, Anne Sommers, Judy Witgenstein, Bonnie Jones, Judy Littleton, and Arlene Bailey.
Special thanks to Allyson R. Abbott for her valuable assistance.

Look for Judy Moore's Other Titles:

Murder in Vail

Somebody Killed the Cart Girl

Football Blues

Airport Christmas

The Holiday House Sitter

The Hitchhiker on Christmas Eve

Chapter One

Victoria couldn't believe it. She thought Brad's invitation to dinner at the Bellagio was extravagant, but she never expected this.

There he was, down on one knee, the black velvet box open, the waiters and other diners waiting expectantly. When he asked her the question, he seemed nervous, more nervous than she'd ever seen him.

A dozen thoughts ran through her mind at once. They'd only known each other for a month. She hadn't met his son. She was thirty-four—what was she waiting for? She'd have to move across the country. Good men were hard to find.

He tugged at his collar as she hesitated, and his cheeks reddened a bit. He stared down at the ring, as if examining it to make sure it was good enough.

The proposal had come as a complete shock, but as Victoria considered it, she knew there was really no question. Brad was the kindest, most caring man she'd ever met, and he made her happy beyond her wildest expectations. She'd never loved anyone as much as she loved him.

The word came out of her mouth before she even realized she'd said it, and suddenly Brad was kissing her, the waiters were beaming, the diners applauding. He took hold of her hand, his hands shaking a little, his face filled with relief, and slipped on the ring, a delicately cut square diamond surrounded by dozens of tiny gleaming diamonds, and even more of them set around the white gold band.

"It's so beautiful," she said breathlessly, holding up her hand to admire the engagement ring.

A relieved smile spread across his face. "I'm so glad you like it—I was afraid you wouldn't."

She glanced up at him in surprise. "Wouldn't like it? It's the most beautiful ring I've ever seen."

Victoria hugged her new fiancé, and wondered excitedly what the future would hold for them. She felt like she was in the middle of a fairy tale and suddenly she was ready for her happily ever after.

The Mother-in-Law

Victoria met Brad in Las Vegas at the national training center for the investment firm where she worked in San Diego. The five-week program was part of the coursework toward becoming certified as a financial planner, a certification she'd finally convinced her boss she was ready to earn. That first morning, she glanced up from her welcome packet to see a blond-haired, suntanned man about her age smiling down at her with the warmest brown eyes she'd ever seen. He admitted that night on their first date that he'd scurried to grab the seat next to her, practically knocking another guy out of the way.

But Victoria's defenses had gone on immediate alert. She realized how attracted she was to his surfer boy good looks and muscular build, and remembered that the last relationship she'd had with a man as good looking as Brad had ended in disaster. He turned out to be a cocky, arrogant womanizer who had cheated on her almost from the day they met.

There was something different about this man, though. It was as if he didn't realize how good looking he was or the impact his appearance had on the opposite sex. He was so down-to-earth, so modest, so considerate. The more she got to know him, the more she realized she could really rely on him, that she could actually trust him. He always seemed to be looking out for her best interests, anticipating her needs, trying so hard to make sure that she was happy.

He'd had to talk her into going out with him that first night. Although she was excited to be in Las Vegas for the first time and felt like exploring, she felt leery of going on a date with someone in the class, someone she would have to see every day if things didn't work out. She'd always been very careful about keeping her work life and her private life separate. As he persisted throughout the afternoon, she considered moving to another seat. She wanted to concentrate on the class.

But he finally cajoled her into accepting a non-romantic buddy date. She did want to see Las Vegas and decided it would be more fun if she didn't have to go alone. So she agreed, but only if they went out as friends, and she paid her own way.

She wasn't sure what to expect, but he surprised her by taking her to the Adventuredome at Circus Circus. They rode the roller coaster, rammed each other with bumper cars, played carnival games, and marveled at circus acts. His playfulness and energy attracted her, and he said the same about her.

Quickly, they became each other's favorite playmate. They zip lined down Fremont Street, hiked in the red rocks of the desert, and went whitewater rafting on the Colorado River. They danced at the hottest nightclubs on The Strip, went to a beach party at MGM Grand, and saw the long-running shows she wanted to see most—David Copperfield, The Blue Man Group, and Cirque du Soleil's Beatles Love. Within days, she felt as though she'd known him her entire life. She found she could really be herself with him, and he said he felt the same way about her.

After a few buddy dates, he insisted they go on "real" dates and was adamant that he would pay. He wined and dined her at many of the top restaurants in Las Vegas. His manners were impeccable. He opened car doors for her, stood when she came to the table, gently protected her as they walked along the crowded sidewalks. She'd never been treated so well in her life.

There was plenty of hand-holding, kissing, and teasing, but she kept him at arm's length for weeks as far as anything more. After her last relationship, she wanted to be sure that this was more than just an out-of-town fling for him. When she finally agreed to spend the night, Brad turned out to be the gentlest, most romantic man she'd ever been with. After one night together, she moved into his suite the next day.

Of course, they studied too. A few times they stayed up half the night quizzing each other on the coursework they'd learned that day. Studying with Brad was fun. He made her laugh like she'd never laughed before. He constantly came up with crazy bets and offbeat challenges for them to test each other. Brad really knew his stuff, almost as well as she did. She'd been a straight A student in school, and her diligent study routine hadn't wavered as an adult. The certification tests to become retirement and financial planners weren't easy, and when the time came for them to take their exams, she was determined they would both pass with flying colors.

The last few days were a whirlwind. Just the two of them, saying their vows at the cute little wedding chapel in Las Vegas, packing up her apartment in San Diego, saying goodbye to her friends. Her boss wasn't happy about losing her, especially since he'd approved the advanced training. But she and Brad put their heads together and managed to get her transferred to his office in North Florida, in Jacksonville, so she would have a job waiting for her when they arrived.

And she couldn't believe her luck—he lived on the beach! She couldn't wait to see his house. Victoria grew up in San Diego but far from the cliffs of the Pacific Ocean. She and her mother lived in a small townhouse in a middle-class neighborhood a good hour's drive inland from the ocean. Going to the beach was a treat, not an everyday occurrence, as it obviously was for Brad.

As an impromptu honeymoon, they played tourist on their cross-country drive to Florida, prolonging stays in Santa Fe, San Antonio, and New Orleans. Now, here she was crossing the Florida line in her loaded down Volkswagen Jetta, ready to start a new life with her new husband.

Husband. The word still hadn't sunk in. She had a husband. She was a wife. Victoria stared at the gold band on her finger and at his as he held the steering wheel. Banded together for life. For as long as they lived. It was so exciting, yet at the same time, it gave her chills to think about it. Everything had happened so fast.

Victoria's only regret was that her mother wasn't there to see it. She would have been so relieved to see her only child settled and happy. If her mother had only been able to hold on for one more year.

Brad must have noticed her melancholy because he reached over and took her hand.

"What's wrong, honey?" he asked softly.

That was another thing she loved about him. He could always tell when she was upset.

"I was just thinking about my mom," she answered, her eyes misting. "I wish she could have met you, Brad. It would have made her so happy to know I found such a wonderful husband."

Brad smiled sympathetically. "I wish I could have met her too."

Victoria stared out the window, picturing the last image she had of her mother, sleeping peacefully in the hospital bed. "She's the only family I had."

"I know," Brad said, rubbing her arm. "But now, you have a whole new family. I can't wait for you to meet Andy. He's going to be crazy about you."

Victoria wasn't even used to being a wife yet and, in a few hours, she would become a mother too. The thought terrified her. Growing up as an only child, she'd never really been around young children.

"I—I hope I know what to do." She had already spent a few sleepless nights worrying about whether her new stepson would warm to her. She had no idea what to say to a five-year-old or how she would entertain him when it was just the two of them alone together.

"Don't worry about it. He's going to love you."

She glanced over at her husband, furrowing her brow. "Do you really think so? You're not just saying that to make me feel better?"

"Of course, I'm not just saying that. You'll be a natural," he assured her. "Don't worry about it. Andy is going to absolutely adore you!"

That made her feel a little better. If Andy was anything like Brad, she didn't think she'd have anything to worry about. "You're sure?"

"Positive! And, don't forget, my mother will be around to help you out too."

Victoria's face darkened and her body tensed. She turned again to stare out the window at the passing pine trees. Her stomach began to churn as it did every time Brad mentioned his mother. Apparently, she had stepped in to help raise Andy when Brad's wife passed away, and she was taking care of him while Brad was in Las Vegas. But he had been kind of vague about her. All Victoria knew was that his mother was a widow, and that Brad was an only child, just like she was. Every time Victoria started to ask more about her, she noticed he changed the subject.

"I'd feel better about it if you'd told your mother about me. What is she going to think? You go off for job training and come back with a new wife?"

Brad laughed and squeezed her hand.

"Don't you worry about my mother. She'll be upset that she couldn't come to the wedding, of course, but we didn't have time to make those kinds of plans. I wasn't leaving Las Vegas without having Mrs. Victoria Reynolds by my side."

Victoria Reynolds. It would take her a while to get used to that WASPY name too. Victoria Verducci was one hundred percent Italian, with intense dark eyes, olive skin, and curly black hair that fell in ringlets down her back. Brad had dubbed her his Italian princess, and she called him her surfer boy. They both looked the part, and their appearance was about as different as two people could be. Maybe the saying that opposites attract really was true.

Victoria was so proud of her Italian heritage. Her mother had seen to that. When Victoria was twelve, her mother had saved up to take her on a trip to the village in Cinque Terre where her grandmother had grown up. She was enthralled with the tiny colorful houses that crowded onto the hills overlooking the Mediterranean and thrilled to learn more about her heritage. Her mother taught her how to cook authentic Italian food, and Victoria liked nothing better than to prepare huge Italian feasts for her friends. She couldn't wait to cook her first one for Brad once they were settled.

The farther they drove into Florida, the more nervous Victoria became. She was used to it being just the two of them. Now there would be a third person in the mix, and a mother-in-law to deal with too. She just hoped they both liked her. But what if they didn't?

The knot that had been growing in her stomach for the last hour felt like it was squeezing the breath out of her. She leaned back in her seat and tried to fall asleep. But as pine tree after pine tree passed by them across Florida's Panhandle on Interstate 10, sleep wouldn't come. She had an uneasy feeling that she couldn't shake. For the first time since she and Brad had gotten married, she wondered if she'd made the right decision.

Judy Moore

Chapter Two

"Victoria!" She felt a hand jostling her shoulder. "Victoria, wake up. We're here."

"Hmm?" she murmured, trying to open her eyes. "We're where?"

"We're only a few blocks from home." Brad leaned over with a big grin and kissed her.

"Home?" Victoria jolted awake. "We're here! You were supposed to wake me so I could get ready. Look at me. My hair's a mess. I don't have any make-up on."

Brad laughed. "You look beautiful. Don't worry about it. You were sleeping too peacefully for me to wake you up."

Victoria scurried to find her hair brush and make-up bag in her purse. She pulled down the visor and started putting on lipstick in front of the small mirror. But she had trouble concentrating on it as she took in her surroundings. Brad told her they were on A1A, the beach road south of Jacksonville. She couldn't believe how gorgeous it was. They passed one beautiful oceanfront home after another, many in mission-style architecture with red-tiled roofs, others in classic Key West style, in the palest of pastel colors with verandahs wrapped around the upstairs and downstairs of the homes.

Between the houses she could see the long shadows of palm trees swaying across the white beachfront of the Atlantic Ocean. The air was filled with the rhythmic sound of waves breaking on the beach and the jingle of wind chimes.

He lives here? she wondered excitedly, running the brush quickly through her tangled hair. My God, it's beautiful. She never dreamed it would be like this.

The next block of beachfront brought mansions that made the Key West-style homes look like guest houses. Towering manicured hedges hid the homes at the end of long driveways, but Victoria managed to get a peek of a huge Tudor house behind one and a cream-colored fieldstone mansion behind another.

When Brad turned into the next driveway, she gasped, "You have to be kidding me."

The Mother-in-Law

Her packed little white car rolled along the palm-tree lined drive to stop in front of one of biggest houses she'd ever seen with a spectacular chandelier hanging from a two-story portico. The mansion had a row of columns across the front in the same gray marble as the rest of the home, and thick white trim framed massive windows across the front. The gray slate, cross-gabled roof was done in a slightly darker shade than the gray of the marble.

But for all its magnificence, the house seemed out of place somehow, a little too formal for its beach setting.

"Welcome home," Brad said, giving her a smile as he took the keys out of the ignition.

Victoria sat in stunned silence, staring at the huge home. Finally, she said, "This is your house? This is where we're going to live?"

Brad caught her by the back of the neck and pulled her toward him. "It's not my house," he whispered. "It's our house."

He nuzzled her neck and gave her a deep kiss.

"Stop," she said giggling, pushing him back. "You're messing up my lipstick."

Judy Moore

She checked her reflection in the visor mirror one more time, touched up her lipstick, and dabbed on some mascara. The knot was back in her stomach.

Brad grinned at her. "You look great. What are you so worried about?"

"This is the first time I'm meeting your mother—and your son. I want to make a good impression."

Brad laughed and shook his head. "You worry too much. You look just as beautiful as you always do."

She tried to smooth her rumpled red tank top and white cutoff jeans. She wanted to look so much better than this when she met them for the first time. First impressions were important.

"I don't want to look like somebody you just picked up along the highway. I'm a mess from traveling all day. I wanted to stop and change before we got here."

"Stop worrying. They're going to love you as much as I do."

With that, he popped open the trunk and got out of the car.

"Daddy!"

Victoria watched as a sandy-haired little boy, a five-year-old version of Brad, flung open the front door and ran down the steps toward the car. Andy wore a

Spiderman shirt and white shorts. He threw his arms around his father's waist.

"There's my little man," Brad exclaimed, lifting his son and swinging him through the air. "I sure have missed you!"

"Me too, Daddy. I want to fly a kite." Andy let go of his father and ran to the porch where he picked up a diamond-shaped Batman kite and hurried to show it to Brad. "See my kite, Daddy."

"Wow. A batman kite. That's nice, Andy, and it would be fun to fly it later. But right now, there's somebody I want you to meet."

Victoria stepped out and walked to the back of the car, trying to calm the butterflies in her stomach.

Brad took her by the elbow. "Andy, this is Victoria."

Victoria wasn't sure exactly what to do, so she crouched down to the boy's eye level and smiled. She didn't know if she should hug him or shake his hand. So she did neither.

"Hi, Andy. That's a very cool kite you have there. Can I fly it too?"

Andy started jumping up and down. "Yes, yes. Right now. I want it to go way up in the sky with the sea gulls."

As Victoria started to respond, a long, dark shadow fell over her and the boy. She shaded her eyes and squinted up through the glaring rays of the sun. Her eyes focused on the unsmiling face of a tall woman with short blonde hair, perfectly styled around a tan, angular face.

"Andrew! You can fly the kite tomorrow. Your father just got here."

"Please, Mimi?" Andy begged, looking up at the woman.

"You heard me. I said no."

Andy looked like he might cry, but he seemed to think the better of it.

"You heard your grandmother," Brad told him. "We'll fly the kite tomorrow."

Victoria thought Brad's mother might speak with a Southern accent, living in Florida. But the woman's voice had a harsh edge to it, with the slightest trace of a European accent. Was it German? Or maybe Scandinavian?

Brad stepped forward to hug the older woman. "Mother, it's good to see you."

"Welcome home, Bradley." She hugged him awkwardly, quickly tapping him on the back and then stepping away.

Victoria stood up, smoothed her tank top, tugged down her jean shorts, and tried to tidy her hair. She may as well have not bothered to comb it with the gusty wind blowing off the ocean.

Brad put his arm around her shoulder. "Mother, I'd like you to meet Victoria."

His mother turned her gaze toward Victoria. This woman was so well put together, so statuesque in her peach-colored designer pants suit. And those icy blue eyes weren't missing anything. Her razor-sharp gaze seemed to pierce the very air. Victoria suddenly felt incredibly self-conscious and out of her element. She just wished she'd had time to change and clean up so she would look more presentable.

Victoria smiled hesitantly and extended her hand.

"It's so wonderful to meet you, Mrs. Reynolds," she said, her words rushing out faster than she intended. "I've heard so much about you."

Brad's mother gave her a quizzical look and a limp hand shake. She nodded to Victoria, and her lips turned up into a semblance of a smile. But those penetrating blue eyes were far from smiling.

She turned to look at Brad questioningly. "Victoria?"

Brad didn't make eye contact with his mother. His eyes darted nervously toward the ocean.

"Yes, Mother," he said hesitantly, clearing his throat. He was usually so confident. Victoria had never seen him unsure of himself.

"Mother," Brad murmured in a voice so low that Victoria almost didn't hear him, "Victoria is my wife."

His mother didn't say anything, but she visibly flinched. Her eyebrows moved together into the mildest of frowns.

Brad rushed to explain, his words falling over one another. "Please don't be upset, Mother, I mean, for us not waiting to have the wedding here so you could attend. We just, just couldn't wait. Victoria is from San Diego, you see, all the way on the other side of the country, and we couldn't bear to be apart. And, they have so many wedding chapels in Las Vegas, it's like, well, you know, almost a cottage industry out there and—"

His voice had become a breathless ramble. Victoria decided to cut in.

"We have beautiful pictures," Victoria said, reaching out to take hold of her new mother-in-law's hand. "Of both the wedding and our honeymoon. I can't wait to show them to you."

The Mother-in-Law

Brad's mother slipped her hand out of Victoria's grip, crossed her arms in front of her, and stood staring stone-faced at her son. Brad glanced around, obviously agitated. Spotting Andy, he picked him up.

"So what do you think, Andy? Daddy and Victoria got married."

Andy seemed confused at first, but then his face brightened.

"Married? Does that mean I have a new mommy now?"

"You sure do," Brad answered with a laugh.

Andy peered up at Victoria, examining her face with those big brown eyes, blinking his thick blond lashes as he studied her face. His expression was so serious, a complete juxtaposition to the spray of freckles across his nose that gave him a mischievous, impish appearance. Victoria wondered what was going on in his little brain as he studied her so closely.

At last, his face broke into a huge smile. "I've been wanting a mommy so bad. All the other kids in kindygarden have one."

When he reached out for her with his little arms, she fell instantly in love with her new stepson. Taking him in her arms, she hugged him tightly, surprised and thrilled that he seemed so happy to have her as his mother. Victoria couldn't help giggling with relief. She had been so worried that Andy would not accept her.

"This is my mommy," Andy announced to his father and grandmother, snuggling his head onto Victoria's shoulder.

Glancing over Andy's shoulder toward Brad's mother, Victoria watched her mother-in-law's face flush a deep pink. The older woman immediately turned her back and strode toward the house.

"Dinner is at six-thirty," she said crisply over her shoulder, right before the front door slammed shut.

Victoria set Andy down and took hold of the little boy's hand. Unnerved by her new mother-in-law's abrupt departure, she whispered to Brad, "I told you we should have called to tell your mother before we got here. Not everyone likes surprises, and your mother obviously doesn't."

It was the first time Victoria had ever spoken to him in that tone. Brad reacted with surprise and a little bit of hurt on his face.

He didn't respond right away, but then answered, "Maybe you were right, honey. Maybe we should have told her. But I'm sure she's just upset that she couldn't come to the wedding. She'll warm up. Don't worry."

Victoria wasn't so sure of that.

"I don't think she likes me," she whispered in a louder voice than she intended.

Andy looked up at her. "Mimi didn't like my other mommy either."

Victoria felt a shudder pass through her. A look of alarm flashed across Brad's face. He immediately reached down and took Andy's hand.

"Race you to the house, buddy!"

Father and son took off, leaving Victoria standing by herself in front of her new home. She'd never felt quite so alone or unsure of what her future might hold. She felt like dashing to the car and speeding away.

Judy Moore

Chapter Three

Brad's house was immaculately furnished, though much more formally than Victoria would have expected for a home on the beach, especially with a five-year-old boy in the family.

If she had been the decorator, she would have filled the home with light, airy rattan furniture, tropical prints, colorful urns full of flowers, and soft, cushiony couches and chairs. The enormous living room was beautiful with high ceilings, wooden beams, and expansive glass windows that looked out onto the swimming pool and the Atlantic Ocean beyond. But the furnishings were so heavy—dark oak with uncomfortable Queen Anne chairs, dark green velvet couches, and huge credenzas topped with ornate silver and glassware. It just came across as so cold and uninviting. With these furnishings,

25

if you weren't looking out the window, you would never guess you were at the beach.

Their bedroom was more of the same. An absolutely gorgeous second-story view of the wide deserted beach, but the king-size, canopy bed was a heavy oak with a red satin covering that looked more appropriate for a Spanish castle. The bureau, dressing table, and huge wardrobe were constructed in the same heavy style.

But the best part of their master suite was that there was an attached sitting room, a little living room really, with a pillowy couch, two comfortable armchairs with matching ottomans, and an old-fashioned settee. They were all made of the same heavy wood, but the pattern of the upholstery was brighter, with a maroon, pink, and light green floral pattern.

Victoria knew she shouldn't complain. This bedroom suite was miles more elegant than any place she'd ever lived. But the décor was just so stiff and stuffy. It didn't fit into a beach setting at all. She hoped she'd be able to start making changes soon, just little by little, so she wouldn't hurt Brad's feelings.

After giving her a quick tour of the downstairs, Brad had immediately collapsed on the bed and fallen asleep. He'd driven nearly nine hours that day, from the cute little bed-and-breakfast on the gulf in Alabama where they stayed the night before. Always such a gentleman, Brad told Victoria to just relax and enjoy the scenery, that he would do all the driving.

She was a little weary, but not so tired that she wanted to take a nap. All day long she'd been thinking about digging her toes into the sand and feeling the warm Florida sun on her back. Unpacking could hold off until tomorrow. She wanted to take a nice long walk on the beach to unwind.

Rifling through her canvas shoulder bag, she found her black bikini with the white polka dots and her long, black wraparound skirt. Slipping them on, she quickly applied some sunblock, pinned her long curly locks on top of her head with a barrette, and grabbed her floppy straw hat and sunglasses.

Quietly closing the bedroom door behind her, Victoria considered taking Andy along with her to the beach. Maybe they could even take along that kite he was so anxious to fly. She looked around for him as she descended the wide, circular staircase, passed through the large dining room and kitchen, and then through a small study and the living room. All the rooms were quiet and empty.

During the short tour Brad had given her, he told her that all seven bedrooms were upstairs. The room where his mother was staying and Andy's room were on the north end of the house, while their bedroom and most of the guest rooms were on the south end. Victoria figured Andy must be up in his bedroom or his grandmother's room playing. Or maybe he was taking a nap. She wasn't about to go looking for him and chance running into her new mother-in-law by herself.

She unlatched the lock to the sliding glass door, stepped out onto the wide coquina stone patio, and gazed at the shimmering oval-shaped swimming pool. Intricate blue and yellow tilework dipped down below the waterline and up onto the edge of the patio surrounding the pool, and two bright yellow umbrellas fluttered in the wind over stone tables and benches. Blue and white chaise lounges and lawn chairs were scattered in bunches around the patio. A large clay fire pit stood at the far end.

Now this was more what she expected from a beach house, she thought with pleasure, as she squinted across the pool, past the sea oats that lined the sandy path to the beach, to the crashing surf of the Atlantic beyond.

Victoria walked around the pool, unhooked the gate separating the property from the beach, and started down the short path. She stopped to take off her sandals before venturing across the finely textured sand that stretched almost the length of a football field to the ocean. The waves foaming at the shoreline were a crystal, transparent blue, and the color grew into a deeper, darker blue in the distance.

Standing at the water's edge with the cold, salty water tickling her toes, Victoria watched a pelican swoop into the ocean for its dinner. She felt like diving in herself, but knew she wouldn't have time to deal with her already out-of-control hair if she went swimming before dinner. So she hiked up her skirt and waded in to her knees. It was the end of April, so the water was still chilly, though much warmer than the cold Pacific currents she was used to. This was her first trip to the East Coast, but she'd read that the Gulfstream-fed Atlantic tides became as warm as bathwater later in the summer.

Alone on the beach, she waded through the surf for a few minutes before starting to walk toward the north along the hard-packed sand of the shoreline, half in, half out of the breaking foam. Tiny coquina shells nosedived into the soft sand with each breaking wave, leaving hundreds of little holes on the shoreline.

As she walked along, flocks of tiny, delicate sandpipers scattered as she approached, while bolder sea gulls stood ground and ignored her. She shaded her eyes and their glanced at the homes of her new neighbors. Most of the houses were two-story, a few were clapboard Cape Cod style, but most had stone or stucco finishes with huge picture windows looking out on the Atlantic. A few were more palatial with mission style or gabled roofs, grand balconies, and perfectly landscaped yards and patios. None, she noticed, were bigger or more impressive than Brad's. Some of the houses were boarded up for the summer, owned, she guessed, by snowbirds who returned to their northern homes to avoid the hot Florida summers.

The name of the beach she wasn't sure of, and Brad kept telling her that she was pronouncing it wrong. It was spelled P-o-n-t-e V-e-d-r-a, and they were at the southern end. She had never heard of it, but she knew they weren't far from a place she had heard of, St. Augustine. She'd studied in school that it was the oldest city in the country and was the place where Ponce de Leon supposedly had discovered the Fountain of Youth.

The location of the house and these other gorgeous beachfront homes seemed pretty isolated. Brad had told her that there wasn't much around for miles. On the other side of A1A, there were just miles and miles of mangroves and cypress brush. She wondered how far they would have to drive to go to the grocery store.

As she wandered along the beach, her mind couldn't help returning to what little Andy had said. *"Mimi didn't like my other mommy either."* She wanted so badly to ask Brad what his son had meant by that. But she'd seen the expression on his face when Andy said it and knew he wouldn't want to talk about it.

They had made a pact early on, on their third date to be exact, not to talk about "exes." Brad said it was too painful for him to hear about hers, and he didn't want to talk about his, didn't want to make her feel bad about anything. The past was the past, he said, and it should stay there. They had both agreed and been true to their word ever since. Still, she was dying to know what Andy meant about Brad's first wife. She had a feeling that she might need to know.

After walking about a mile, she turned around and headed back. She couldn't believe she'd been on the beach for nearly forty-five minutes and hadn't seen another soul. But as she approached Brad's house, she noticed an older man a little farther down the beach sitting in a lawn chair with a fishing pole anchored in the sand.

She bypassed Brad's house and walked another fifty yards or so up to the fisherman, who looked to be in his late seventies or eighties. He was wearing Bermuda shorts, a T-shirt, and a floppy beige hat.

"Catch anything?"

He glanced up at her, but didn't reply. Instead, he held up an old blue pail with three fish in it. One was still flopping around.

Victoria stared at the fish. They weren't too big, a foot or so at most. She didn't know anything about fishing, but tried to look impressed.

"Wow. What kind are they?"

"Just whiting."

Victoria nodded. She'd never heard of that kind.

"Is that going to be your dinner?" she asked with a smile.

The man nodded. "If you catch 'em, it's only right to eat 'em."

His pole jerked, and Victoria watched as he reeled it in. The fish on the line was tiny, only about five inches long, so he unhooked it and tossed it back into the surf.

The Mother-in-Law

As he started baiting his hook again, Victoria asked him, "So, do you live in one of these houses?"

He jerked his thumb toward a long, yellow ranch-style house with a huge picture window and a big wraparound deck. The house was three doors down from Brad's. "My wife and I have lived here for thirty-five years. Wouldn't live anywhere else."

His gaze rested on her for a moment. "I've never seen you out here before. You visitin'?"

Victoria shook her head and extended her hand. "I'm Victoria, your new neighbor." She pointed to the large gray mansion. "I just moved in this afternoon."

A cloud seemed to pass over his face. "You're moving in there?"

Victoria noticed his change in demeanor. "Well, yes. Maybe you know my husband? Brad? We met in Las Vegas and were married last week?"

"Oh yeah," he said in a friendlier tone. "I know Bradley. Haven't seen a lot of him lately."

"What's your name? I'll tell him we met."

"I'm William. I see the little one that lives there out here all the time."

"Andy."

"Yes, little Andy. He's a cute one. Too bad about—"

33

"Victoria!" A loud shout pierced the serenity of the quiet waterfront. Victoria glanced around to see Brad standing on the patio, his hands cupped around his mouth. Andy was by his side.

"I'd better run," she said. "Don't want to be late to dinner on my first night. Nice to meet you, William."

She started to walk away, but then remembered something he had said and turned back.

"William, you were about to say, 'Too bad about.' Too bad about what?"

He gave her a long look and then focused his attention back on his fishing pole.

"Never mind. It's not for me to say," he said. "You'll find out soon enough."

Chapter Four

Andy came running across the patio and wrapped his arms around Victoria's legs.

"Where have you been, Mommy? We were looking for you," he asked brightly, peering up into her face.

She reached down, tousled his hair, and felt a burst of happiness. She couldn't believe he was already calling her Mommy! She was beyond thrilled that he had warmed to her so quickly. But it also felt strange. Now and forever more, she had a new name. Mommy.

"I just went for a long walk down the beach, Andy. I haven't been to the beach in a very long time."

Brad walked over and hugged her, leaving his hand resting on her shoulder.

"I told you," he whispered, nodding his head toward Andy.

35

She whispered back, "You were right. I'm just so thankful."

She reached down and put her arm around Andy's shoulder, leaned her head on Brad's, and the three of them stood gazing out at the ocean. The shadows of the beachfront homes crossed the sand as the sun descended deeper and deeper into western sky behind them. This was Victoria's favorite time of day at the beach. She felt more at peace than she had in days, especially with her new little family gathered around her.

"So, what do you think of our beach?" Brad asked her after a few moments of looking out at the idyllic scene.

"It's absolutely gorgeous. And so deserted. I walked a mile that way and didn't see a soul." She nodded her head toward the north.

"A lot of people have winter places here and go back home for the summer. We're one of the few who are here year round."

Victoria glanced to the south, but saw that the fisherman had packed up and gone inside. "I did meet one of your neighbors, William, from the down the beach."

"I know Mr. William," Andy piped up. "Sometimes he plays catch with me. And one time he let me help him catch a fish!"

Brad smiled down at his son. "William is a great guy. I've fished with him many times. He's pretty quiet, and keeps mainly to himself, but he doesn't miss much. Always knows what going on in the neighborhood."

"He was starting to tell me—" Victoria began.

A sharp voice behind them broke their peaceful family scene. "He's an old busybody. Always into everybody else's business. Don't listen to a word he says."

Victoria turned around and immediately let go of both Brad and Andy. Brad's mother made her feel so self-conscious, like she was an outsider, trespassing into their world. Her mother-in-law seemed to suck all the warmth out of the air.

Victoria could feel Brad's mother's critical eyes scanning her bathing suit and bare midriff. She felt Mrs. Reynolds' gaze come to rest on the small rose tattoo on the front of her shoulder, the one Victoria had gotten the week after her mother died as a remembrance. Her mother's name was Rose, and getting the tattoo had just felt right.

A look of disdain flashed across the older woman's face, but it disappeared as quickly as it had come. "Dinner is almost ready," she announced, glancing at her watch. She lifted an eyebrow at Victoria. "I assume you'll be changing?"

Victoria's hand flew to her throat, and she suddenly felt as if she were doing something wrong. "Oh, yes, yes, of course. I'll hurry."

"Please do. I always plan dinner for 6:30 sharp." Mrs. Reynolds put her arm around Andy's shoulder and pulled him toward her. "It's important to teach children to be on time. It's irresponsible not to be."

Victoria felt the heat rise in her cheeks. She quickly excused herself and scurried across the patio, into the living room, and up the stairs to change. She glanced at her watch. Only five minutes until dinner. What could she throw on quickly so that she wouldn't immediately be known as the "irresponsible" new parent?

Unzipping her suitcase, she dug down beneath her blue jeans looking for an appropriate outfit. Her mother-in-law was wearing a really attractive belted pant suit. Did they dress for dinner? Brad was wearing nice khaki pants and a new golf shirt, and even little Andy had on long pants. She pulled out her favorite sundress, but it was wrinkled. And strapless. After seeing Mrs. Reynolds' expression when she noticed Victoria's tattoo, she felt self-conscious about exposing her shoulders. She needed something with sleeves.

The panic kept rising as she looked at her watch and realized she had only three minutes left before 6:30. Digging farther down in the suitcase, she found a short-sleeved pink jersey top that wasn't wrinkled. She grabbed it, pulled it on, and decided on her best pair of jeans. Quickly, she ran a brush through her hair and dabbed on some lipstick. Then, she literally ran down the stairs, arriving at the table out of breath.

Brad and Andy were already seated, and Mrs. Reynolds was placing the food on the table—broiled salmon in a luscious-looking lemon sauce, boiled red potatoes, a steaming bowl of spinach, and hot rolls. Victoria slid into the seat across from Brad and tried to calm herself. Any appetite she had was gone, vanished from her flight down the stairs.

She'd felt Mrs. Reynolds giving her a cursory inspection as she circled the table to take her seat, her mother-in-law's eyes resting on Victoria's jeans. She wished she'd had time to press one of her skirts or a pair of dress pants, but she hadn't had time to do anything.

What was she thinking spending so much time on the beach? How could she have been so inconsiderate when she knew her mother-in-law was cooking dinner for them?

The table was set impeccably with sterling silver cutlery and beautiful dishes that had a delicate flower petal design. They looked very expensive. Victoria wondered if they might be Wedgewood. She noticed Andy's dishes were plastic. Not a surprise. Who would risk setting a five-year-old's place with expensive china? As Mrs. Reynolds poured white wine into crystal wine goblets, Victoria wondered if this was the way they dined every evening, or if this was a special celebration to welcome them home.

"Everything looks so beautiful," Victoria told her mother-in-law. "And that salmon looks scrumptious."

Mrs. Reynolds nodded without smiling. "Yes, well, I hope it tastes as 'scrumptious' as it looks," she said, putting what sounded to Victoria like a sarcastic tone on her choice of adjective.

Victoria wondered if they would say grace before the meal. She suddenly realized that she didn't even know if Brad was religious. How crazy was that? Victoria was Catholic but rarely attended any more other than an occasional holiday service. She couldn't remember even asking Brad if he practiced a religion. They were married at a nondenominational Las Vegas wedding chapel, and the subject of religion had never come up.

No grace was said, and Mrs. Reynolds served each of them a large piece of salmon, and then picked up the bowl of potatoes and passed it to Brad. Brad spooned some potatoes onto Andy's plate, and then onto his own, before handing the bowl to Victoria. Next, Mrs. Reynolds passed the bowl of spinach to Brad, and he began to shovel a spoonful onto Andy's plate.

Andy scrunched his nose. "I don't want any. I don't like spinach."

Mrs. Reynolds peered at him, her hawk-like eyes laser focused on her grandson.

"No arguments, Andrew. You must eat your spinach."

Brad flexed a bicep at his son and smiled. "Don't you want to grow up to be big and strong like Popeye?"

Andy crossed his arms across his chest and pouted. "No. I don't like spinach. Don't make me eat it, Daddy."

Brad hesitated, obviously unsure what to do. His mother shifted her gaze from her grandson to her son. Brad seemed to wilt under her stare.

"Now, Andy, your grandmother said you have to eat your spinach, so you have to eat it. It's good for you and will help you grow up big and strong like me."

Andy crossed his arms even tighter, his face turned red, and he shook his head fiercely. "No!"

"Andrew!" the stern voice came from the end of the table. "Don't you raise your voice to your father and me!"

A tear started to roll down the little boy's cheek.

Victoria's heart broke for him. She didn't like spinach either when she was a child and couldn't imagine being forced to eat it. Her mother never made her eat food she didn't like when she was growing up. She couldn't remain quiet.

"You know, I hate to say it, but I didn't like spinach when I was little either."

Andy blinked away a tear and looked up at her, a hopeful glint in his eye. Brad gave her a little frown and shook his head at her. His mother shifted her stare to Victoria.

"I'm sure your mother made you eat your spinach, Victoria. I always made Bradley eat his."

Brad flexed both arms jovially, his muscles rippling. "And look how it paid off."

But Andy hadn't taken his eyes off Victoria across the table. She winked at him.

"Well, actually, my mother never made me eat food I didn't like. But that didn't mean I didn't have to eat vegetables," she said, looking directly at Andy. "We just tried different kinds until we found some I liked."

"I want to try different kinds," Andy said, a look of hope in his eyes. "Just not spinach."

Brad glanced at his mother who was glaring at Victoria.

"Children must learn to eat what they are given," she said. "It's not for them to pick and choose. They don't know what's good for them."

Victoria shrugged. "Well, I like spinach now, and I'm not sure I would have if it had been forced on me. When I was Andy's age, I liked peas and carrots, so I ate a lot of them."

"I like carrots," Andy chirped.

Mrs. Reynolds pressed her lips together and stared down at her plate. She began folding and refolding her napkin. "Well, that's not the way Bradley was raised, and that's not the way Andrew is being raised either, is it Bradley?"

Both women turned to stare at Brad who immediately began to fidget uncomfortably. He seemed to shrink under his mother's gaze and didn't say anything for several moments. Then he cleared his throat.

"Well," he began, "since the spinach is cooked tonight—not carrots—and Andy needs to eat a vegetable with every meal, Andy, tonight you have to eat your spinach. We'll have carrots tomorrow and let you try out some other vegetables in the future."

"No," Andy cried, jumping out of his chair and running around to hug Victoria around the waist. "Don't make me eat the spinach, Mommy."

He looked up at her beseechingly. She glanced across the table at Brad, not sure what to do.

Brad stood up, came around the table, and picked up his son. "Now, Andy, sit down and eat your dinner like a good boy. I had to eat my spinach when I was a little boy, and you do too."

As Andy sat whimpering in his chair, Brad forced him to take a bite of spinach. Mrs. Reynolds took a sip of wine and gazed at Victoria with a little smile.

"You'll learn that this family has its own ways of doing things," she said.

Chapter Five

Victoria couldn't sleep that night. Her mind kept going over and over what had turned into a confrontation at the dinner table over the spinach. What was she thinking giving her opinion like that during their first meal together? She had just met Brad's mother and barely even talked to the woman. And then to question her child-rearing techniques? Victoria knew nothing about raising children, and Mrs. Reynolds had raised Brad and was now taking care of Andy.

She did seem very stern, though, and it seemed a little cruel to make the child eat something he didn't like. But maybe you had to be firm when raising children, especially rambunctious little boys. And, for heaven's sake, look how well Brad turned out. He was such a gentleman, so considerate and well-mannered.

Andy was adorable too, such a well-behaved little boy with the exception of the outburst at dinner. After he settled down and ate a few bites of spinach, Victoria noticed his table manners. He used exactly the right utensil, sat up straight and tall in his seat, and made a point of not talking with his mouth full. And he always said please and thank you. Mrs. Reynolds had obviously spent a lot of time with him, teaching him the right etiquette. Victoria could picture him growing up to be just like Brad.

Brad's mother had warmed up a little too as the dinner went along. Victoria apologized again for not waiting to get married so that she could attend, and she seemed to accept that Victoria never would have given up her job and moved to Florida with Brad if they weren't married.

His mother was extremely reserved and sat silently when Brad brought out his laptop and showed her photos taken at the wedding and on their honeymoon. She asked a couple of questions and displayed mild interest in a few of them. But she did compliment their wedding picture—Victoria in the long white sheath satin dress she'd bought in a Vegas boutique with a bouquet of pink peonies, and

Brad looking dashing in his rented tuxedo with one of the flowers as a boutonniere.

Victoria made a vow to herself to be more careful about what she said in the future until she got to know her new mother-in-law better. She didn't have much experience dealing with extended family—it had always been just her mother and her. She had a tendency to be a little blunt and blurt out exactly what was on her mind without always thinking about the impact of her words on other people. She needed to work on that, especially with people who were older and more sophisticated, like her mother-in-law. She wanted so badly to start off on the right foot, to fit in. Brad's mother definitely seemed a little harsh and would take some getting used to, but Victoria was determined that this new relationship would be a good one. It had been so nice of her to take care of little Andy for the whole month while Brad was away at training.

The next morning, Brad woke her early to tell her he was leaving to drive Andy to kindergarten and then run a few errands. It was Friday, and they didn't have to start work until Monday. So they had a few days to unpack and settle in before her new job began. Victoria was excited and anxious about the transfer and meeting a whole new group of associates. She just hoped she would be able to make some friends at the office.

But she didn't want to think about work right now. She snuggled under the sheets for a while, thinking back about all the fun times they'd had in Las Vegas. She stretched out her arm in front of her and looked at her rings. She still couldn't believe she was married. And to such a perfect man. She felt like the luckiest woman in the world.

She yawned, threw back the covers, and decided to take another walk on the beach. And maybe a swim in the pool too. She just wanted to relax and enjoy more of that glorious Florida sunshine. After driving cross-country, it felt wonderful just to be out of the car.

She searched her suitcase for her other bathing suit, this one a pink, high-cut one-piece. After she changed into it, she surveyed herself in the mirror and frowned. There was no denying she'd put on a few pounds in Las Vegas, especially in her hips. She'd always been curvy, with big breasts and a nice-sized derriere that, thankfully, was in fashion thanks to celebrities like Jennifer Lopez and Kim Kardashian. But she'd like to shed a few pounds. Maybe some swimming and walking on the beach would do the trick.

The Mother-in-Law

She threw on a knee-length white terrycloth cover-up, grabbed a big fluffy pink towel from the towel rack, and headed downstairs. Entering the kitchen, she thought she might find Brad's mother there. But the kitchen was empty, except for a note on the counter. *"There is coffee in the pot, bagels in the bread box, and cream cheese and fruit in the refrigerator. Please help yourself. Then rinse your dirty dishes and put them in the dishwasher. Madeline."*

Hmmm. Madeline. So that was her mother-in-law's name. She had been wondering what she should call her. Mrs. Reynolds seemed so formal, but "Mom" definitely didn't fit the bill either. She guessed this might be Brad's mother's way of letting her know what she would like to be called.

Victoria glanced around the large kitchen. She never seen so many cabinets, all in the same dark oak as everything else in the house. How nice and bright the kitchen would look if the cabinets were lighter. She visualized a whitewashed pine that would be so much nicer for a beach house.

But it was a great kitchen, grand really, with beautiful dark hardwood floors, granite counter tops that went on forever, an enormous island in the middle, and a

49

homey eat-in breakfast table in the corner. A huge iron rack hung from the ceiling over the island, holding a dozen cast-iron skillets, as well as all sizes and shapes of pots and pans.

Victoria opened several of the cabinets until she found the same set of dishes they had used for dinner the night before. She took down a cup and saucer, filled it with coffee, and added two spoonfuls of sugar and a splash of milk.

Then, she pulled open the door to the large black refrigerator. The bagels and cream cheese were front and center, waiting for her. That was nice of Mrs. Reynolds, she said to herself. She noticed the food in the refrigerator and the dishes in the cabinets were as organized and pristine as the rest of the house. With a grimace, she remembered the state of her own apartment in San Diego before she moved. She wasn't a slob, but she was far from neat. Her mother used to kindly call it "the lived-in look." She wondered what her new mother-in-law would think if she'd ever seen it.

Victoria toasted her bagel, spread more cream cheese on it than she knew she should, and carried it and her coffee out onto the patio. It was calm today, just a wisp of a breeze, so she stretched out on a chaise lounge, set the food on a wrought-iron end table next to it, and began nibbling on her bagel. The weather was perfect—in the mid-eighties and not a cloud in the sky.

After she finished her bagel, Victoria pulled off her cover up, tiptoed on the hot pavement to the edge of the pool, and tested the water with her big toe. A little cool, but not too bad, especially on a warm day like this. She pinned up her hair with a barrette and waded into the shallow end. She wasn't one to dive into the pool all at once, so she took her time getting wet, just a little bit at a time. Once she was wet, she started doing the breast stroke, keeping her head above water, trying to keep her hair dry.

She'd taken swimming lessons as a child, but only one three-week session. So she wasn't the best swimmer. They didn't have a pool at the complex where she lived in San Diego, so swimming had never seemed like much of a priority. She knew the rudimentary strokes, but was told by her teacher that she splashed too much.

And her instructor was right. Before she knew it, her hair was soaked. She gave up trying to keep it dry and dove underwater. She tried to swim the length of the pool underwater, but it was too long and she wasn't able to make it the whole way.

Judy Moore

Her barrette came loose, so she took it out and tossed it onto the patio. Then she rolled over on her back and started floating. She felt her long hair spread out in the water around her face like a big black headdress. She must look like Medusa, she thought with a giggle. Closing her eyes, she basked in the sunlight, feeling like she didn't have a care in the world. The Florida sun felt so good on her skin. It felt hotter here than in California. Brighter too.

"Victoria!"

Victoria snapped out of her reverie and bolted upright to find her mother-in-law standing by the side of the pool with her hands on her hips. She wore black bicycle pants and a black sports bra—her body tight, tan, and muscular. She looked amazingly fit.

"Oh, hi, uh, Mrs.—"

"What are you doing? You mustn't swim in the pool without wearing a bathing cap. All that hair will clog the drain." She sounded disgusted.

Mortified, Victoria quickly gathered up her long, soggy curls and held them ponytail style behind her head. She waded toward the steps.

"Oh, I'm so sorry. I didn't think."

Her mother-in-law didn't answer, but from the expression on her on face, Victoria could tell the woman thought she was mentally deficient.

She tried to explain. "I—I so rarely swim in a pool that it, uh, my hair, it just didn't occur to me."

Her mother-in-law quickly crossed the patio to a wooden chest in the corner, opened it, and after searching for a moment, pulled out a white bathing cap.

"Here," Mrs. Reynolds said, handing the latex cap to Victoria as she stepped out of the pool. "You can have this one. It's my old one."

"Oh, well, uh, thank you. I hope all my hair will fit in this. I have a lot of hair."

Mrs. Reynolds lifted her eyebrows as she peered at Victoria's hair. "You certainly do."

Then her gaze moved downward, scanning Victoria's figure in her bathing suit. The older woman's eyebrows knitted together as if she'd seen something distasteful, and she looked away. Victoria immediately felt uncomfortable, not to mention huge standing next to the slim woman.

"I really am sorry," she told her mother-in-law again.

Brad's mother straightened her shoulders, continued to frown, and didn't say anything for several moments. "Well, please remember next time," she said finally.

Victoria felt like disappearing into a black hole, but she knew she needed to win her new mother-in-law over, no matter what. She had to try to engage the woman in conversation, to be friendly. Wrapping her towel around her hair like a turban, she sat down on the end of the lounge chair and patted the lawn chair next to her. Mrs. Reynolds seemed surprised, but begrudgingly sat down on the edge of it, looking like she was ready to bolt at any second.

"Wow," Victoria said. "You are in absolutely amazing shape. Have you been bicycle riding?"

"Bicycle riding?" The question seemed to offend her. "Why in the world would you say that?"

"Well, your outfit. Aren't those bicycle pants?"

Mrs. Reynolds glanced down at her pants. "These are my running shorts. I run twelve miles on the beach every day. I compete in half marathons."

Victoria was impressed. Half marathons? Wasn't a marathon twenty-six miles? So she ran in races that were thirteen miles long. That was incredible for a woman her age. Brad's mother looked so youthful and fit, but she had

54

to be in her mid-fifties, didn't she? Brad was thirty-two, two years younger than she was. His mother must have had him when she was pretty young.

"Well, you look fantastic. So fit. And half marathons. I can't even imagine!"

The older woman obviously liked the compliment and showed the first hint of a genuine smile that Victoria had seen from her. But then she gave Victoria another visual once over, not even trying to hide her inspection.

"What do you do for exercise, Victoria?" Her voice sounded harsh, and Victoria noticed the slight European accent again.

Victoria glanced down at her arms and legs—smooth and silky, but not a muscle to be seen.

She giggled nervously. "Well, exercising isn't really my thing. Although I did enjoy my long walk on the beach yesterday. I'd like to do more of that."

Her mother-in-law shook her head. "No, no. That's not nearly enough. You have some weight to take off, so you must do something more aerobic to burn more calories."

Victoria flinched at the words. Had she heard the woman right? *Did my mother-in-law just call me fat?*

She glanced down at her hips. She's never thought of them as being flabby, but maybe they were. They did look a little fuller than usual, probably from all those dinners in Las Vegas. Maybe Brad's mother was right. Maybe she did need to lose some weight.

"Yes," her mother-in-law continued, fixing her eyes on Victoria's thighs. "It's important to keep your body fat percentage low. Especially as you get older."

She does think I'm fat, Victoria thought, jutting out her bottom lip. And she just called me old too. Does she know I'm two years older than Brad?

Victoria wasn't sure if the age comment was a dig or if she was just being sensitive. But there was no mistaking that Brad's mother was sniping at her weight.

Chapter Six

The topic of conversation was beginning to upset Victoria so she decided to change the subject.

"I'm not sure what I should call you," she said shyly. "Mrs. Reynolds seems so formal. I noticed you signed your note Madeline. Should I call you Madeline?"

Her mother-in-law stared at her for a second, a surprised expression on her face. Then she shrugged as if she didn't care. "Madeline will be fine."

There was a long silence before Mrs. Reynolds glanced at Victoria's coffee cup and breakfast plate. "Are you finished with those?" she asked, standing up.

"Oh, yes, yes," Victoria said, hurriedly picking up the cup and saucer to hand them to Brad's mother. She was so tense that her hand slipped, and the cup went crashing to the ground. It broke into several pieces.

Victoria cringed and made a sharp intake of breath. Her mother-in-law stood there as if she were in shock, staring down at the shattered cup.

"That's Wedgewood," she said finally, shooting a condemning look Victoria's way. "Do you know how much that cup was worth?"

"Oh no. I'm so sorry, Mrs.—Madeline," Victoria said. "I can't believe I did that."

Victoria felt like such a fool. She reached down and started picking up pieces of the broken cup. Suddenly, she felt a sharp pain and blood spurted out of her thumb.

"Ouch!" she squealed, grabbing the pink towel she had wrapped around her hair and holding it on the wound.

"No!" her mother-in-law yelled. "You're getting blood on one of my good towels."

Still in pain, with blood continuing to flow out of the cut, Victoria took the towel off her hand and held it out to Brad's mother. "I'm so sorry," she began. "It hurt so much I just didn't think."

Her mother-in-law grimaced and waved the blood-stained towel away.

"The damage is already done."

She took hold of Victoria's hand and examined the wound, frowning. "Not much of a cut."

The Mother-in-Law

After instructing Victoria to put added pressure on the wound, Mrs. Reynolds left the patio to get a broom. When she returned with a broom and dustpan, she began silently sweeping up the pieces, a look of irritation spread across her face.

"Here, let me do that," Victoria offered, reaching for the broom.

"No," Mrs. Reynolds answered, pulling the broom away. "You've done enough already. I'll do it."

Victoria started ringing her hands, yelping when the motion pulled at the wound. "I'm so sorry. Please let me pay to replace it, them. The cup and the towel."

"Replace what?" Brad's friendly voice came from the patio door. What a welcome sight he was, standing there in his madras Bermuda shorts, light blue golf shirt, and leather flip flops.

"Oh, Brad. I'm so sorry. I broke one of your Wedgewood coffee cups." She was visibly upset, and he noticed immediately.

He crossed the patio in a few steps and pulled her into a hug. "Don't worry about it, sweetheart. It's just a cup."

His mother glared at him. "A Wedgewood cup. We don't use our Wedgewood for morning coffee."

59

Victoria's eyes started to tear up as she explained to Brad. "I didn't know what cup to take. This was the same pattern we used last night at dinner. No one was home this morning."

"Like I said, 'It's just a cup,'" Brad said, sending a look of rebuke his mother's way. He hugged Victoria closer. "I don't want you to get this upset about a piece of china. Don't worry about it."

Victoria unwrapped her hand and held it up for her husband to see. Blood was still dripping down her wrist. "And then I cut my hand trying to clean it up and got blood on one of your mother's best towels."

Brad examined the cut. "My poor baby," he said soothingly. His touch was so tender that Victoria immediately felt better.

"You may need a few stitches. That's a deep cut."

His mother made a dismissive sigh and told them to move so she could sweep under them.

"I don't think I need stitches," Victoria said as she stepped out of the way. "Just an antibacterial cream and a bandage."

Brad turned toward his mother. "Mother, Victoria is hurt. Don't worry about sweeping up the cup right now. Go get her a bandage, for heaven's sakes."

His mother stopped sweeping, glared at him, and then took the broom and dust pan into the house. She slammed the sliding glass door shut behind her.

A tear rolled down Victoria's cheek as she looked up into Brad's sympathetic eyes. "I can't seem to do anything right. I think your mother hates me."

He pulled her into his embrace and stroked her hair. He didn't say anything for several moments as he held her.

"My mother can be a little severe at times," he said softly, "And, trust me, nobody knows that more than I do. But she doesn't really mean anything by it. Once you get to know her better, you'll get along fine."

Victoria wished she could believe that. But, somehow, she just didn't see that happening and found herself starting to pity her husband for what must have been a miserable childhood.

"What was your mother like while you were growing up?" she asked curiously as she continued to hold her hand in the air to stop the bleeding. "What she hard on you?"

Brad shook his head. "Not really. I mean, I was careful not to rock the boat. You just have to know what upsets her and avoid those things. Then, she's pretty easy to get along with. Overall, she has always been very supportive of everything I've been involved in."

"Supportive how?"

"Well, for instance, I played baseball. Remember, I told you I played from the time I was in Little League through high school. I don't think she ever missed a game."

Victoria lifted her eyebrows in surprise. "I'm having trouble picturing your mother as a Little League mom."

Brad hesitated and frowned a little. "Well, I wouldn't exactly call her that. She kind of stayed off by herself. Didn't mingle too much with the other moms."

He seemed to cringe a little as other memories came back. "Actually, I seem to remember her getting into some arguments with the other parents. And actually the coaches too, now that I think of it. But she was always super supportive of me. You know, telling me I was the best player on the team. That kind of thing."

"I'll bet you were good," Victoria said, smiling up at him. "I wish I could have seen you play."

Brad grinned. "I was pretty good, I guess. But definitely not the best. I think my mother was the only one who thought that!"

The Mother-in-Law

The sliding glass door opened with a loud crack, and Brad's mother appeared holding a tube of cream and a gauze bandage. With an annoyed expression, she glanced quickly down at Victoria's cut again, handed Brad the first aid supplies, and then went back inside the house without saying a word.

Judy Moore

Chapter Seven

Brad held her hand like she was a delicate porcelain doll as he bandaged the long cut on her thumb. Then he tenderly brought her bandaged hand to his lips and gave it a soft kiss.

"All better now?" he asked.

She smiled and nodded. Now that her sweet Brad was here with her, all her troubles vanished. She didn't want her time alone with him to end.

"Come for a walk with me down the beach," Victoria urged her husband. "I don't want to go back inside the house right now."

Brad glanced over at the sliding glass doors. "Um, sure. Just let me give my mother a holler to tell her that we're going."

He stepped over to the patio door and called inside that they were leaving for a walk. There was no response. At least Victoria didn't hear one.

Brad extended his hand. She took it with her unbandaged one.

"So, what did you do this morning?" she asked him, as they emerged from the path through the sea oats and turned to walk south on the sand. The tide was in, and the beach was much narrower than it had been the evening before.

"Well, I dropped Andy off at kindergarten, and then got my hair cut and ran a couple of errands."

Victoria stopped in the sand. "Let's see," she said, standing back to examine his hair. "It doesn't look much different to me."

Brad laughed, flashing his perfect white teeth. "Well, I know you like it long, so I didn't let them take off too much. But I usually wear it a little shorter."

"I remember it was shorter when I first met you," she said with a giggle. "I thought, 'Who is this preppy guy who's so determined to sit next to me?'"

He chuckled. "I guess I did look pretty preppy. But this preppy guy was ready to fight off anybody who tried to horn in on the exotic Italian princess with the long, jet black hair. The prettiest girl I'd ever seen."

"Really? The prettiest?" she asked, giving his hand a squeeze.

"The absolute most gorgeous woman I've ever laid eyes on. Beautiful, inside and out."

"And you're my handsome surfer boy," she said, noticing how much lighter his hair appeared with the sun beating down on it, and how it stood out against his deepening tan.

She leaned her head on his shoulder as they walked. He always knew exactly the right thing to say to her to bring her out of the doldrums. It sounded trite, but she couldn't believe she'd been able to find someone who actually was her soulmate. How lucky was she?

"Oh look," she cried. "Here comes William. I met him yesterday."

The older man was shuffling through the sand, loaded down with his lawn chair, fishing pole, bait box, and pail.

Brad let go of Victoria and jogged over to help him.

"Here, let me grab that chair for you, William." The two men shook hands and slapped each other on the back like long-lost friends.

"I haven't seen you in months, Bradley. Where have you been hiding yourself?"

"I've been out in Las Vegas in training," he said, adding with a broad grin. "Got myself a new bride!"

Victoria couldn't help but smile at the pride in his voice.

"We met yesterday afternoon," William told him. "I'd say you got yourself a good one."

He seemed much friendlier today. Victoria guessed he was one of those people who was just aloof with strangers,

"I've known this young man since he was smaller than little Andy," William told her. "He and I have caught many a fish together."

Brad laughed. "Yep. William here taught me how to fish from the shore, and how to body surf too come to think of it."

Victoria frowned. That didn't make sense. How could William have taught him those things?

The men continued talking, while Victoria mulled over what she'd just heard in silence.

"You should get your rod and reel and come on out and fish with me one of these days," William said to Brad. "There's some big ones out there."

The Mother-in-Law

Brad nodded and agreed. "I need to get my license renewed, but that's a great idea, William. We'll plan on it."

They chatted for a few more minutes before saying goodbye, and Brad and Victoria continued walking down the beach. As soon as they were out of William's hearing distance, Victoria stopped to ask Brad the question that was nagging at her.

"Brad, I don't understand. You lived in the house growing up? I thought you bought it when you were older."

"No," Brad said, shaking his head. "I've lived in that house my whole life."

Now Victoria was really confused. She let go of his hand and took a step back.

"But your mother. What about your mother? Where does she live?"

Brad stared at her for several moments and then turned away. He stood with his back to her, his hands on his hips, staring down at the sand.

"Brad?"

He turned around slowly, but kept looking down in the sand.

"I haven't known how to tell you this, Victoria. I've put it off as long as I could. Everything's been so wonderful between us, I didn't want to put a damper on things."

"Tell me what? What are you saying?"

"Um," he couldn't seem to get the words out, and he still wasn't making eye contact. "Well, uh, actually, my mother lives in the house. She'll be living here with us."

Victoria felt all the happiness, all her excitement for the future drain out of her in an instant. That critical, unfriendly woman would be living under the same roof with them? This could not be happening. It would be challenging enough to have her in the same town, but in the same house!

"Living with us? In our house?" she murmured. "Please tell me you're kidding."

He continued staring at ground and started making a design in the sand with his big toe.

"Unfortunately, I'm not," he said finally. He hesitated and grimaced. "And, well, uh, actually, it's the opposite of that. We'll be living with her. She owns the house."

Victoria gasped. Her house? Brad had led her to believe it was his house. How could he have done that?

She had been looking forward to having her own house, decorating it, cooking for Brad, raising his son.

How could he possibly expect her to live in his mother's house, follow his mother's rules? How could he ever have thought that would be all right? Oh no. This was not possible. This was not going to happen.

"No, Brad. No."

Brad shot her a tortured look. "Please, Victoria. It won't be forever, and she'll be a big help with Andy while we're at work."

Victoria's head was spinning. She felt like she was going to be sick. "Why can't we get our own place? It doesn't have to be fancy. It doesn't have to be big."

Brad shook his head. "No, that wouldn't be fair to Andy. This is the only home he's ever known, and he loves it here, with the beach and everything."

"Andy will get used to it. Little kids don't care where they live as long as they're with their parents. He can still visit here."

Brad just stood there with his eyes closed, running his hands through his hair. Then, he covered his face with them.

"Please, Brad. I don't understand."

"I've never lived anywhere else. I don't want to live anywhere else."

Victoria couldn't believe what she was hearing. Who was this weak man? Where was the Brad she'd fallen in love with?

"But, Brad—"

"Mother doesn't like to be alone. Can't stand being alone. She wants me here. She needs me here."

She felt like shaking him. He couldn't be serious.

"Brad, when children grow up, and especially when they get married, they leave home. It isn't always easy for mothers, but it's something they all have to deal with when the times comes. And, eventually, they adjust to it—even like it."

"Not my mother."

"Brad, seriously. This is ridiculous. We need to move away from here and get a place of our own."

Brad started pacing and shaking his head. "No, no, no. We can't. I can't. You don't understand. You just don't understand."

Victoria was fuming. "Well, why don't you explain it to me then, Brad?"

His face was flushed. She had never seen him this upset.

"My mother grew up in Austria," he began. "Her parents died when she was very young, about Andy's age. She was put in an orphanage and mistreated horribly. They beat the kids, and there was little food or heat. One winter, she almost froze to death. Now, she can't stand to be alone. She needs her family around her. I thought she would go crazy after my father died. I—I have to be there for her."

Victoria tried to process everything she was hearing. Of course, she felt sympathy for Brad's mother and what she'd been through, but did she have to insist that her adult son live with her? Or was this more about Brad's guilt about leaving her?

She made an effort to respond with as much sensitivity as she could. "Brad, I'm really sorry to hear what happened to your mother when she was a child, but a lot of people go through hardships when they're young and they overcome them. It's not fair of her to put this on you. Who knows? Maybe if she got out some, she might meet someone and marry again."

Brad looked at her as if she'd lost her mind.

"My mother would never marry again. She's always said my father was the love of her life, and she would never consider it. He saved her from all that, from that horrible life she was leading. He was in his last year of law school, studying international law in a foreign studies program in Vienna, when they met. She was only nineteen."

Victoria continued to protest that his mother needed to learn to cope with being alone, as all widows do. But she felt like she was fighting a losing battle, and she was beginning to feel exhausted from it. Brad had an answer for everything.

Finally, she said, "Brad, I'm all out of arguments. Is there nothing else I can say? Isn't there any way we could move into a place of our own?"

"I can't. Just believe me when I say, I can't."

She peered out to the horizon, not really focusing on what she was seeing. She felt as if she'd gone into shock. How could this be happening?

"Brad, why didn't you tell me this before we got married?"

His face froze. He looked like he might break down.

"I was afraid. I was afraid I'd lose you, Victoria. You mean so much to me. I couldn't take that chance. I was so in love."

Part of her wanted to reach out and comfort him. The other part wanted to slap him silly.

He held out his arms and pulled her into a hug. "I can't lose you. You're my whole world."

She leaned away from him—she couldn't look at him.

"Please, Victoria. Please. Just tell me you'll try. We'll work it out. It won't be so bad once you get used to it. Please, for me. Tell me you'll try."

She found herself wishing she didn't love him as much as she did, because if she didn't, she would have been on the next plane back to San Diego.

Looking at his troubled face as he waited for her response, a feeling came over her that she'd never felt before, like something precious was about to be destroyed. It hurt to the core.

Not able to meet his eyes, she looked out over the ocean and whispered to him, "I'll try."

Judy Moore

Chapter Eight

After they returned to the house, Victoria immediately left Brad downstairs and ran upstairs to their bedroom. She undressed quickly and stepped into the huge marble shower. It was the fanciest shower she'd ever been in with a marble corner seat and five different shower heads. She turned all of them on full blast, as hot as she could stand it. She had managed to hold in the tears on the walk back on the beach, but if she'd uttered two words, she couldn't remember what they were.

Now the tears came, in torrents, and leaning back on the tile wall as the spray washed over her, she found herself sliding down the wall and crumpling to the floor, sobbing as hard as she had when her mother died.

How could this be happening? This time yesterday, everything had been so perfect. She had married the man of her dreams, they got along so well, had so much fun together, had never even had a cross word. They were on their way to a beautiful new life together in Florida. She'd given up everything she'd ever known, everything that made her feel comfortable and secure to make a leap of faith to marry this man and follow him across the country.

She felt betrayed. How could he force this woman on her like this? This critical woman who clearly didn't like Victoria and went out of her way to make her feel uncomfortable. Yes, she was his mother, but mothers were supposed to know their place in their adult children's lives. They didn't force themselves into it. Her mother would never have done such a thing. Force her grown child to live with her?

Or was it Brad? Was he too afraid of hurting his mother? Was he so tied to her apron strings that he would do anything she asked? Or was he just plain spoiled? Was he so used to this wealthy lifestyle that anything else seemed second rate?

Victoria glanced around the luxurious shower. She didn't need to live like this. Who cared about nice things if you weren't happy? She would take her happy middle-class life over all this wealth any day of the week if she and Brad and little Andy could live away from here, by themselves. Why was Brad being so resistant?

In Florida, real estate prices were so much lower than in California. They wouldn't be able to afford a place that approached this one, but they could afford to buy a nice enough house for the three of them. Maybe not on the beach, but close by.

Her chest felt like it had a crushing weight pushing into her ribs. What was she going to do? Her mind was blank. She couldn't think. It felt like every ounce of energy had left her body. She took a few deep breaths and pushed herself slowly up into a standing position. Wiping away her tears, she turned off the shower jets. She wrapped herself in one of the plush gray towels piled on the shelf outside the shower and wound another one around her hair.

When she stepped out of the bathroom, she found Brad sitting on the edge of their bed, anxiously waiting for her.

"Baby, I'm sorry," he said, taking hold of her hands and pulling her toward him. "Please don't be upset with me. We'll make it all work. You'll see."

Victoria buried her head in his chest and didn't respond. She didn't know what to say. She still felt like she was in shock.

Brad seemed to take her silence as disapproval and kept talking. She'd begun to notice that when he was nervous, he talked too much.

"Just think, we won't have to worry about Andy after school or during the summer while we're at work. Day care expenses can be really high, you know. Mother will be here to pick him up from school and take care of him in the afternoon. It will be so much better for him. He won't have to be with strangers. And when we want to travel, to get away just the two of us, Mother will be here to take care of him. She is awfully good with him, you know, and—

"Ok, Brad! I get it."

She pulled away from him, crossed the room to the vanity table, and sat down. Unwinding the towel around her head, she started drying her hair with it.

"Victoria, please don't be mad."

She sighed wearily. "I'm not mad, Brad. I'm just disappointed. Incredibly disappointed."

He began pacing again, something she'd also begun to notice he did when he was upset.

"It won't be forever."

Victoria eyes brightened, and she stopped drying her hair to look at him.

"Really? How long?"

He frowned and hesitated. "Well, I'm not sure. But it won't be forever. I'll work on it. I promise."

Victoria pursed her lips and turned her back on him, staring at her reflection in the mirror. She felt like such a weakling. She wanted to stand up for herself and scream, "Hell, no!" she wasn't going to live in his mother's house. She wanted to scream at him, "You coward! How could you not tell me this before you asked me to marry me?"

But she couldn't bring herself to do it. She could see that Brad was trying, trying so hard, and that he was suffering too. She had taken him for better or for worse, hadn't she? Marriage was about compromise, wasn't it? What kind of wife would she be if at the first hint of trouble she gave up?

She let out a long, tired sigh, closed her eyes, and said, "Okay."

Brad rushed across the room, took her by the shoulders, and peered hopefully into her eyes. She could see how much he loved her—she could actually feel his love. It radiated from him. She couldn't do anything to hurt this dear man. She loved him too much.

"Brad, I told you I'd try and I will. I promise I'll try to make it work. But, Brad, your mother has to try too. She can't be so," she searched for the word, "harsh."

Brad's face lit up, and he started bouncing around the room like a teenager.

"I'll talk to her, I promise. She just takes a little getting used to, that's all. She'll warm up to you, I know she will. I mean, what's not to love? Before long, the two of you will be the best of friends. I just know you will–"

"Okay, Brad," Victoria answered, cutting him off. She couldn't foresee ever being "besties" with Mrs. Reynolds. "Just be sure to talk to her—today."

Brad came up behind her, wrapped his arms around her, and looked at their reflection in the mirror. "Let's go to St. Augustine tomorrow. I want to show you my favorite city. Just you and me. And Andy too if you want."

Victoria looked at his reflection. "I would love to get out of the house and go to St. Augustine. You've told me so much about it. And, of course, we'll take Andy. I love that little boy already."

Brad's face actually shone, as if sun beams were reflecting off of it. Other than when he said, "I do," Victoria didn't think she'd ever seen him so happy. It must be such a relief for him, she thought, to have the secret of where they would be living—and with whom—out in the open. She could see that he wanted all the people who were most important to him to be living peacefully under one roof. She was beginning to understand that about Brad and, above all else, Victoria found herself wanting Brad to be happy. If living here with his mother made Brad happy, then she would try her best to be happy here too.

At dinner that night, it was apparent that Brad had kept his promise and spoken to his mother. She was actually almost pleasant the entire meal, and gave them some suggestions of places they might enjoy in St. Augustine. She even asked how Victoria's thumb injury was and complimented the floral summer dress Victoria had unpacked and ironed for the meal.

Victoria noticed that the table was set with everyday stoneware that night, not the Wedgewood. So maybe Madeline did just have it out for a welcome home dinner—or possibly to impress her new daughter-in-law. Even more likely, Victoria guessed, maybe her mother-in-law wasn't going let her anywhere near her good china ever again.

Maybe this will work out, Victoria told herself after they finished eating. If Brad's mother continued to act the way she did during dinner, Victoria could see it possibly working. There was no question that it certainly wasn't ideal, but Victoria decided to try to focus on the positives rather than the negatives. The house they would be living in was gorgeous, it was right on the beach, and Mrs. Reynolds—Madeline—was like a babysitter, cook, and housekeeper all rolled up into one. Of course, there were some negatives, but as long as she and Brad worked through any problems together, how bad could it be?

Chapter Nine

Victoria awoke with a fresh attitude. She pushed all negative thoughts from her mind, and couldn't wait to see St. Augustine. She decided to wear her favorite blue-and-white striped sundress with the wide sailor collar, her broad-brimmed straw hat, and new straw sandals.

As soon as they were able to convince Andy to sit still long enough to down a bowl of cereal, they pulled out onto the beach road and headed south toward the nation's "Oldest City." Strapped safely in the middle of the backseat, wearing a Smurf T-shirt, white shorts, and blue-and-white sneakers, Andy bubbled with excitement, especially about playing "goofy golf" on a miniature golf course that had a big pirate ship in the middle of it.

St. Augustine was less than a half hour ride down A1A, through the little oceanside town of Vilano Beach, and then across the Intracoastal Waterway on the Vilano Bridge. As they came down off the tall bridge onto San Marco Street in St. Augustine, Andy started bouncing up and down and clapping his hands when he saw a colorful carousel in a little park.

"I wanna ride the merry-go-round!" he squealed.

Brad smiled at him in the rear-view mirror and pulled into the first parking space he could find. The three of them held hands as they crossed the small park to the revolving carousel under the big red-and-white striped tent. They stood in a short line waiting for the carousel to stop so they could have their turn.

"I used to ride this merry-go-round when I was a little boy," Brad told Andy. "My daddy would bring me here just like I'm bringing you!"

Andy looked up at Victoria and giggled. "But you didn't have Mommy with you then."

Brad and Victoria both laughed. "Well, no, but I had my mommy, Mimi, your grandmother."

Victoria tried to picture a younger Madeline Reynolds having a carefree day in St. Augustine, climbing onto the merry-go-round to take a spin. Somehow, it just didn't register. Victoria whispered to

Brad what she was thinking while Andy played with another little boy in line as they waited.

"Well, to tell the truth," he told her chuckling, "Dad would drop Mom off at the dress shop up the street and then bring me here by himself. We'd ride it four or five times and then go pick her up. She wasn't really the merry-go-round type."

Now that she believed.

"You know, Brad, you haven't told me much about your father. It sounds like the two of you were close."

"Very close." Brad glanced away and his voice took on a softer tone. "I've always wondered how my life would have been different if he had lived."

Immediately understanding the pain a parent's death could bring, she told him she was sorry. "How old were you when he passed away?"

"Twelve. I was off at summer camp in North Carolina when I got the news." He stared at the ground, his face coloring a bit, and Victoria reached out to give him a comforting rub on the arm.

"How did he—"

"Just died in his sleep. They said it was a heart attack. He was only forty-two. Can you believe that?" He shivered. "Hope I didn't get that gene."

Judy Moore

Victoria cringed thinking about that possibility as the carousel slowed to a stop and several children and a few parents poured off.

Andy grabbed Brad's hand. "C'mon, Daddy, let's go!"

Brad started ahead with his son, looking back over his shoulder at Victoria.

"You're coming too, aren't you?"

She grinned at them. "Heck, yeah! Hey, wait up, Andy."

Andy beamed back at her as Brad lifted him into the air onto a white pony with a blue mane and a bright pink stirrup. He climbed onto the yellow horse next to Andy, and pointed to the black one with a green mane behind them for Victoria.

Victoria hadn't been on a merry-go-round since she was kid, but feeling the moist Florida air hit her face, and listening to the loud ring of the circus music in her ears, took her back to happy times in her childhood when her mother took her to the Southern California Fair.

By the time the ride was over, she felt giddy. She wasn't sure if it was from dizziness or happiness. Walking on wobbly legs, she took Brad's arm as they stepped back onto terra firma.

88

Andy spotted a huge wooden jungle gym across the park and took off running for it. Brad and Victoria followed him and found a wooden park bench under a towering oak tree, draped with Spanish moss. Brad put his arm across the back of the bench, and Victoria leaned her head on his shoulder. They watched Andy as he charged up wooden walkways, tunneled through long plastic tubes, climbed up the sides of wooden turrets, and swung on a rope swing, dropping into the soft sand below.

Once, when Andy was at the highest point of the wooden tower, Victoria thought he was going to fall. She leapt up from the bench and dashed underneath to catch him. He just laughed at her and climbed down, but Victoria couldn't believe how quickly she had developed protective feelings for her new little stepson. She had been so afraid he was going to hurt himself.

Brad chuckled and teased her, "It can be pretty scary being a parent, can't it?"

After Andy had his fill of the wooden play land, they walked down the street to catch an open-air sightseeing train, pulled by a red locomotive engine. Andy was enthralled. "Toot, toot!" he cried out, pumping his arm each time the train crossed an intersection.

The train shared the road with several horse-drawn carriages as it maneuvered its way past the Fountain of Youth to the waterfront where several quaint two-story inns overlooked the bay. Then the train turned the corner onto the beautiful oak-filled town square with its charming central gazebo. The tour took them past all of St. Augustine's major downtown sites, the Spanish government buildings, Lightner Museum, numerous historic churches, and the city's centerpiece—the turn-of-the-century Ponce de Leon Hotel built by Henry Flagler that was now Flagler College.

As the sightseeing train waited for a stoplight to change, Victoria watched a young bride and groom and their wedding party pose for pictures in front of the arched brick columns, tall clay-colored towers, and bubbling fountains of the hotel turned college, what the tour train driver called the finest example of Spanish Renaissance architecture in the state of Florida.

Seeing the beautiful bride in her beaded, strapless gown laughing with her bridesmaids in their identical coral-colored dresses, and the handsome groom posturing with his tuxedoed attendants, brought a lump to her throat as she thought about the wedding she'd always dreamed of having when she was growing up. It would have been a lot like this one—a big wedding party at a beautiful venue on a sunny spring day. Not that she didn't love every second of their hurried Las Vegas nuptials, but she'd had so many dreams of her perfect wedding growing up.

Watching her as she observed the wedding party, Brad seemed to know exactly what was going through her mind.

"I know we didn't have the perfect wedding, honey, but maybe someday we'll have a big formal renewal of our vows. How would that be? Maybe on our fifth or our tenth anniversary?"

She squeezed his hand. He always knew the perfect thing to say when she needed cheering up.

"That would be nice," she said. "Maybe right here in St. Augustine."

When the train circled around to the old fort, the Castillo de San Marcos, they decided to get off and take a tour of the huge coquina rock monument, built nearly 500 years before by the Spanish to defend St. Augustine. They roamed across the five-pointed rooftop of the fort, gazed over its turrets at the Matanzas Bay beyond, explored its living quarters, and wandered around its vast grounds. The cannons fascinated Andy, and he was disappointed when he found out one wouldn't be shot off while they were there.

After about an hour, they started getting tired and decided to catch the next train that came along to take them back to their car. While they sat in the grass, waiting for the train, a big hay-colored golden retriever came bounding up to them, his attached leash dragging behind him. Andy jumped up and started petting the dog.

"I want a doggie so bad," he said. "Daddy, do you think we could get a dog someday?"

Brad grimaced. "Uh, I don't know about that, Andy. You know Mimi doesn't want a dog in the house messing things up."

Andy hugged the dog. "I wish we could have one."

"I had a dog when I was growing up," Victoria told them. "An Irish setter named Gumdrop. I loved that dog so much."

"It would be nice," Brad said wistfully. "I've always thought it would be fun to have a dog."

The golden retriever's owner came running across the grass and thanked them for holding the dog. Victoria wasn't sure if Andy was going to let go of the dog's neck or not, but he finally released it. What a shame Madeline wouldn't allow a dog in the house. They had the perfect house for it on that deserted beach.

Andy was thirsty so while Brad played tag with him on the lawn, Victoria found a vendor and bought three Cokes.

Andy eyes widened when she handed him his drink. He haltingly accepted the can of soda, looking sheepishly at his father. Brad shrugged.

"It's okay this once," Brad told him conspiratorially. "We just won't tell Mimi. It'll be our secret. She'd be mad at me for drinking a Coke too."

Victoria was confused. "Oh, I didn't know. Isn't Andy allowed to drink Cokes?"

Andy and Brad both shook their heads in unison.

"Oh, I'm sorry. It never occurred to me."

"It's okay, Mommy," Andy said, taking her hand. "I like Coke. My teacher gave us some once in kindygarden on play day. But when Mimi found out, she got mad at my teacher, and we were never allowed to have any again."

Yikes, Victoria thought, suddenly feeling pity for Andy's teacher.

She lifted an eyebrow at Brad. "So, let me get this straight. You don't drink Coke either?"

He covered his mouth with his hand, trying to hide a laugh.

She leaned forward and whispered, "Funny, I seem to remember you drinking Coke all the time out in Las Vegas."

He laughed again and whispered back, "Just not in Mother's house."

Victoria cringed at the statement as Andy tugged on his father's sleeve. "What are you whispering about? Mimi told me it's not polite to whisper."

Just then the train pulled into the parking lot. "Saved by the train," Brad said, winking at Victoria. But Victoria was irritated by the reminder that they were living in "Mother's house," and ignored him, taking Andy's hand and helping him onto the train. When Andy stepped up, the Coca Cola can bobbled in his hand and nearly half of it spilled on his white shorts.

"That's great," Victoria said to herself, grimacing as she tried her best to clean up the stain on Andy's shorts. "Evidence that I broke another one of Mimi's rules."

Andy was just as upset as she was.

Chapter Ten

But the Coke-spilling incident was soon forgotten a couple of blocks later when the train passed by Ripley's Believe It or Not museum and its garish advertisements. Andy immediately started begging to go inside.

"My friend Joey at kindygarden got to go, and he said it was sooooo much fun."

Brad shook his head. "No, Andy. Not today. Let's wait until you're a little older. We can't do everything in one day. You'll enjoy it more when you're a bigger boy."

The long sightseeing train continued to wind its way back to the depot when they passed another of St. Augustine's most popular attractions, the Old Jail. Victoria pointed it out to Andy.

Andy started bouncing up and down on his seat. "I wanna go. I wanna go to the Old Jail. That's where they put the bad people."

"That might be fun," Victoria agreed, elbowing Brad in his side for confirmation.

But instead of the assent she expected, Brad's face seemed to freeze and drain of color. She'd never seen such a strange look on his face.

"Brad? Are you okay?"

He looked away and didn't answer her question.

"Brad?"

He turned back, the odd expression still on his face. "Oh, uh, sorry. What did you say?"

Victoria cocked her head and eyed him quizzically. "I asked if you wanted to take Andy to the Old Jail. It sounds like fun."

Andy chimed in again, and began tugging on his father's arm. "Daddy, I want to go to the Old Jail. I want to go to the Old Jail."

In an instant, the look vanished and the old Brad reappeared again. "No, son, like I said before, we can't do everything today. Anyway, I'm hungry, aren't you? Let's go down to St. George Street and get some lunch."

Andy pouted momentarily, but his hunger seemed to get the best of him. "Yay! I want pizza."

Brad smiled, obviously relieved. "I know just the place. Best pizza in St. Augustine right in the middle of St. George Street."

At the end of the route, they jumped off the train, returned to their car, and drove to a parking lot near St. Augustine's most historic street. They walked hand-in-hand down the middle of the pedestrian walkway, exploring the specialty shops, souvenir stores, and quaint restaurants and taverns of the old Spanish town.

"I can understand why this is your favorite city," Victoria told him as they walked. "It has so much charm, and there's so much to do."

"I knew you would like it," he said, obviously pleased. "I see many, many visits to St. Augustine in our future."

"And next time," he added, "we'll come at night and go on the Ghost Tour!" Grinning fiendishly, he leaned over and started tickling her.

"Stop," Victoria protested, wriggling to get away from him. "You know how ticklish I am."

Andy burst out laughing and joined in the fun. "Tickle, tickle, tickle," he said, as he reached up, tapping his fingers on her waist.

Victoria broke their grip and skipped ahead laughing. "Stop, Stop. I can't take it anymore."

They found the Italian restaurant and ordered a large pepperoni and sausage pizza that turned out to be one of the best pizzas Victoria had ever eaten. Then, it was time for the promised "goofy golf," so they drove across the historic Bridge of Lions to Anastasia Island and the beaches.

As they passed St. Augustine's famous Alligator Farm, Brad gave Victoria a surreptitious glance and put his index finger to his lips warning her not to read the sign. Victoria took the hint, and neither of them said a word as they passed the attraction, home to hundreds of the dangerous reptiles. She had no desire to see the huge toothy creatures either. Living her entire life in California, she'd never seen one in person, and didn't care if it stayed that way. Luckily, Andy was in the back seat totally distracted with a coloring book Brad had bought for him in a gift shop on St. George Street and didn't notice as they sped by the huge signs advertising the zoological park.

The Mother-in-Law

A few minutes later, they reached the beachside miniature golf course with the big pirate ship in the middle that was Andy's favorite. Andy was in heaven, though he knocked the ball so hard on the first few holes that it landed on the green Astroturf carpet of the hole in front of them. Luckily, no one was in the line of fire.

Brad was patient and showed Andy how to hold the club, as well as just how much backswing to take to be sure his son didn't take out any tourists who were out for an afternoon of putt-putt. Andy loved the instruction from his father and was eager to please. Victoria could see that Brad had a lot of experience playing golf. Obviously, she thought, growing up in this part of Florida where there seemed to be a golf course on every corner. He made a hole-in-one on just about every other hole, even one when he had to carefully time his putt to miss an oar swinging down from the ship.

Victoria had never played the game—she'd never taken up any sports—but she felt content leaning back on Brad's chest as he wrapped his arms around her and demonstrated the putting motion. She even managed to make one hole-in-one on the miniature course, which earned her a little peck on the cheek from both of her boys.

On the drive home, Andy fell asleep, and Victoria leaned her head against the window of the passenger door and almost did too. But her mind wouldn't rest. It had been such a perfect day and couldn't have gone any better. But despite all the good feelings, her mind kept going back to that one odd moment of the day. What was Brad's strange reaction to the Old Jail all about?

Chapter Eleven

Victoria's new job started on Monday, so she spent most of Sunday unpacking, not that she had much to unpack. She'd sold most of her furniture and home furnishings in San Diego before she left. The rest she'd given to her friend Shelly to sell at her next garage sale, which seemed to have become an every weekend occurrence, almost a part-time job for her friend. Shelly promised to send her a check of the proceeds and then give the rest to charity.

So Victoria had mainly clothes—several stacks—as well as her jewelry box filled primarily with costume pieces, a box of books she couldn't bear to part with, several framed photographs and picture albums from her childhood, and a few assorted odds and ends. She also had a box filled with all of her photography equipment.

Photography had become her passion, and her only real hobby. She couldn't wait to get out on the beach and take some pictures of Brad and Andy. She already had several ideas for some natural shots that she wanted to take. With their sand-colored hair cut almost exactly the same way, their high cheekbones, and deep-set brown eyes, they could be father-son models in any magazine. Andy looked like Brad's "mini me."

She'd unpacked her smaller Nikon camera to get some "honeymoon" photos on their trip east and was especially proud of the ones she taken in the French Quarter in New Orleans and on the San Antonio River Walk. There were three or four that she wanted to blow up and frame.

While Victoria was unpacking, Brad's mother had been helpful, almost pleasant, clearing out closets and bureaus to give her plenty of space. Madeline even let her use a beautiful oak bookcase from one of the guest rooms and helped Brad carry it into their master suite for her books. Victoria didn't know what Brad had said to his mother, but whatever it was, it seemed to have worked. She appeared to be making a real effort to accept Victoria. Her manner was still brusque, but her words didn't have the critical edge they had earlier.

But Victoria couldn't help overhearing part of a conversation that was far from pleasant between Brad and his mother when they were in the guest room getting the bookcase and apparently thought she couldn't hear. Her mother-in-law was grilling Brad about the Coke stain on Andy's shorts, and it was clear she was very unhappy about it.

"She didn't know, Mother," Victoria heard Brad tell her. "One can of Coke isn't going to kill him. A half can. He spilled the rest."

Mrs. Reynolds said something back to him, but Victoria couldn't hear it, and her mother-in-law never did confront her directly about letting Andy drink the banned substance. So, thank God for small miracles, she said to herself, and had to admit that Brad's mother did seem to be trying to keep the peace. But Victoria couldn't help but wish it was just the three of them, away from here, in their own house. She'd try to make the situation work for Brad, but it wasn't going to be easy.

That afternoon, Victoria and Brad took Andy out on the beach and finally flew the kite with him. Victoria took along her big Sony camera with the super zoom lens and took some cute father and son shots of Brad and Andy running through the sand as they tried to get the batman kite into the air. She also took what she thought were a few terrific photos of some pelicans flying in formation.

Andy started giggling when she lay on her back in the sand behind him to get a shot from the ground up of him with his kite flying high in the air. Then Brad came over and swung Andy onto his shoulders, the kite still flying high in the sky. Victoria started snapping them from different angles. Her husband certainly made a photogenic model with his deep tan, muscular arms, and flat stomach. And he looked the part of the perfect devoted father, flashing his wide smile and gazing adoringly up at his son. One of these pictures, she decided, she would enlarge and frame as a gift for Brad on Father's Day. It was just around the corner.

She glanced back at the house and saw a silhouette of Mrs. Reynolds standing at the window, the drapes pulled back, watching them. It made an interesting composition, so Victoria aimed her zoom lens at the house and took the picture. Brad's mother looked like such a lonely figure standing at the window that Victoria felt a pang of guilt. Maybe they should have invited her to join them on the beach. She hadn't really thought about it, and Brad didn't mention it. After a month of taking care of Andy, she was probably feeling left out now that they were home. Victoria realized guiltily how inconsiderate it was of her not to realize that.

She wandered over to Brad. "Shouldn't we have invited your mother to come out here with us?"

He seemed surprised at the question and shrugged. "If she wanted to come out, she would have come. No big deal."

"But maybe she feels left out because the three of us are always doing things together. I don't want her to feel excluded."

"She's probably just trying to give us some alone time. It's nice of you to think of her, but don't worry about it, Victoria. You worry too much."

Victoria sat down on the beach towel, carefully placed the camera back in its case, and looked back at the window. The drapes were closed now, her mother-in-law gone. Maybe Brad was right. Maybe she did worry too much. But next time, she would make a point of asking Madeline to come along.

Anyway, she had other things to worry about. She was starting to become nervous about starting her new job the next day. She had been so comfortable in her office in San Diego. After working there for six years, she'd gotten to know everyone in the office very well.

She liked them, and they liked her. But it took time to develop those kinds of work relationships. What if the people in this office didn't like her? What if they resented her because Brad had helped her get the job?

For the most part, she was thankful that Brad would be in the office too and that they would be working together. But she'd always been such a stickler for keeping her work life and her personal life separate. That would be an awful lot of togetherness. She just hoped it wouldn't cause problems.

As she sat musing about her new job, listening to the waves crash a few feet in front of her, a huge chunk of sand landed in her lap, startling her. She jerked her head up to see Brad standing next to her, a boogie board under each arm. Hiding behind him was Andy, giggling and peeking around at her with a mischievous grin on his face. She picked up a handful of sand and jumped to her feet.

"Did you do that, Andy?" she teased. "I'm gonna get you!"

He squealed and took off running down the beach. When Victoria caught up to him, she plopped the handful of sand right in the middle of his back. He collapsed in the sand, rolling with laughter.

"Bet you can't get me," Victoria challenged, running into the surf.

Andy jumped up and dashed after her, and within seconds they were having a splashing battle.

Brad waded into the waves next to them. "Who wants to go boogie boarding?" he asked.

"Me, me, me!" Andy shouted, raising his hand.

"Not me," Victoria said, wading to the shore. "I'm going to be a spectator. I want to see my surfer boy in action."

For the next hour, Victoria relaxed on a beach towel watching Brad slide along the breaking surf on the shoreline doing some impressive tricks and miraculously keeping his balance on the mini surfboard. She took out her camera again and started snapping away.

Enjoying the show, she could only imagine how good he was on a real surfboard. "He really is my surfer boy," she said to herself.

Brad held Andy's hand as the little boy tried to balance on the boogie board. Andy struggled at first and kept falling off. But Brad was very patient with him, and by the end of the hour, he had Andy bending his knees with his arms far apart, gliding across the surf like a little pro.

Victoria threw back her head and let the fading afternoon sun warm her. She felt gloriously happy. Could life be any better than this?

Chapter Twelve

Victoria and Brad drove the half-hour commute into work in his big tan SUV. The office was in Jacksonville, not far from the beaches, in a huge office park with manicured lawns, tree-lined walkways, and several ponds with fountains spraying up from them. It actually reminded Victoria a lot of her office location in San Diego. Maybe the parent company, Sherwood Investments, looked for this type of office environment for all of their locations, of which there were dozens across the country.

Before going inside, Victoria smoothed her dark blue gabardine skirt, pulled on the matching jacket over her white silk blouse, and slipped on her navy blue pumps. Brad looked handsome in his grey suit and blue silk tie that she'd bought for him in Las Vegas.

When the couple walked into the lobby of the financial investments office, they heard a few shrieks of "They're here!" and found themselves quickly surrounded by the friendly faces of about two dozen office workers. Someone thrust a bouquet of red roses into Victoria's arms.

It was all a blur to her, but everyone seemed to love Brad and seemed so happy for them. Several of the women gushed over her ring and wanted to know details of the wedding. Everyone had chipped in and bought them a $500 gift certificate to a big department store in Jacksonville as a wedding gift. Victoria felt overwhelmed by it all but thrilled with the reception and relieved that her new co-workers were so friendly and welcoming.

The Jacksonville office was a little smaller than the one where she worked in San Diego, but not that much smaller. There seemed to be about thirty full-time employees. Brad took her into a large office to meet her new boss, a woman of about 50 named Sharon Walsh, and proudly introduced his "new bride." Victoria wasn't sure if she was one of the people who had greeted them in the lobby, but she quickly found out that she wasn't.

"Sorry, I was on the phone with corporate so I missed the celebration," she told them, giving Brad a hug.

She shook Victoria's hand and asked them a couple of polite questions about the wedding before shooing Brad out of her office.

Sharon talked to Victoria for a half hour, explaining the parameters of the job and having her sign some paperwork. There was no need for the full orientation to Sherwood, since Victoria had been working for the company for six years in San Diego. Then her boss took her on a tour of the office, introduced her to every employee, described their job, and let Victoria know how her job might intersect with theirs in the future. As they moved along from one cubicle to the next and she was inundated with information, more than one person jokingly told Victoria, "You'll be quizzed on all this when the tour is over."

Everyone she met was extremely nice and seemed so excited that Brad, a widower with a young son to raise, had married again. A few people asked her if she'd met Andy yet. While she realized that Brad was well-liked in the office, which didn't surprise her at all, it did surprise her that Andy was popular with them too. Apparently Brad had brought him into the office a few times, and the five-year-old had turned on the Reynolds charm that he'd obviously inherited from his father.

Only one employee seemed unfriendly and aloof—a rail thin woman with short black hair and one of the darkest tans Victoria had ever seen. She barely turned around to greet Victoria. Initially, Victoria thought she might just be busy, but later she noticed that the woman kept staring at her while she was being introduced around at the other cubicles.

Victoria's biggest surprise of the morning came when the tour was over, and they reached an empty office at the end of the hallway.

"This is your office, Victoria," Sharon announced. "We're expecting you and Brad to pass your certification tests with flying colors, and you'll need privacy when you're meeting with clients."

Victoria was stunned—and elated. She just assumed she'd be getting a cubicle as she'd had in San Diego. In all the years she'd been working, since she graduated from San Diego State with her business degree, she'd never had an office of her own. Her new office wasn't that big, and the furniture was nothing to brag about, but it had a window—and a door! So it felt like heaven to her. Things were definitely looking up.

When she was left alone in her new digs, the first thing she did was to arrange the roses in a vase one of her co-workers had filled with water for the flowers and set them on a corner of her desk. Then she took a framed wedding photo out of her shoulder bag and put it on the shelf of the bookcase next to her desk.

She set the picture at several different angles, and then couldn't decide whether it looked right on the shelf or if she should move it onto her desk. Contemplating the best position for the photo with her head tilted and her fingers over her lips, she her a soft tap on the glass that looked out into the center of the office.

"Knock, knock," a friendly female voice said.

"Oh, hi," Victoria said, crossing the room to shake the hand of a tall, slender woman with shoulder-length auburn hair. "I know we met earlier, but I'm sorry, I don't remember your name. I'm afraid I don't remember anyone's except Sharon's"

"And Brad's, of course," the woman teased. "I'm Kate, your next door neighbor."

Kate strode into the office and leaned forward to get a better view of the wedding picture.

"You made a gorgeous bride," she said with a smile. "You both look so happy."

"It was whirlwind," Victoria said. "But when it's right, you know it."

"Well, I want to hear all the details," Kate said, returning to the door. "Let's go to lunch soon."

"I would love to," Victoria told her. "I feel like it's my first day on the job, but I've worked for the company for six years. At least the work will be familiar."

"What office were you in before?"

"San Diego," Victoria replied. "How about you? How long have you been with Sherwood?"

"Only three years with Sherwood," Kate said. "But I've been in the business since I graduated from college. So, it's been about twelve years."

She must be about my age, Victoria calculated. Based on first impressions, Victoria liked Kate's easy breezy personality. She hoped they would become friends.

"Well, if you need anything, just let me know. Just tap on the wall," Kate added with a laugh.

Victoria asked Kate for the directions to the supply closet, and Kate volunteered to show her the way. Victoria spent several minutes looking through the drawers of supplies and filled an empty stationery box with notepads, pencils, pens, paper clips, a stapler, and Post-It notes.

On the way back, as she passed Brad's office, he waved her in. His office was quite a bit larger than hers— he'd worked there for almost five years and was a manager now. She sat down on the edge of an office chair at a small work table in the corner and set the box of supplies on the table.

"So how's your first day going?" he asked her. "What do you think of your office?"

"I love it! It's so nice to have four walls that go all the way up to the ceiling. And I have a nice view of a big oak tree outside my window. I only had a cubicle in San Diego."

Brad smiled smugly. "I worked my magic for you. When I called in last week, they told me that Dave Jacobs was retiring. I asked them to hold his office for you. Friday was his last day, so it worked out perfectly."

"I could kiss you!" she said. He opened his arms, inviting her to do so.

She quickly held up her hands in front of her face. "Oh no, none of that in the office. I was lucky to get this transfer, and I'm not going to mess it up."

Brad laughed. "I know. I know. Just kidding. But is your work husband allowed to take you to lunch?"

"Of course. Just not today," she said with a grin. "My new boss is taking me."

"Well, I just can't win, can I?"

"I'll pencil you in for tomorrow."

Brad laughed. "I'm going to hold you to that!"

Chapter Thirteen

The next few weeks went by quickly. Victoria immediately fell back into the work routine and found everything about the job to be similar to what she had been doing in San Diego. So at least there was comfort in familiarity.

When they pulled into the driveway every evening about six o'clock, Andy would be sitting on the porch waiting for them. Always so excited to see them, he would come bounding off the porch and grab one or both of them by the hand, anxious to tell them about a school project he did in kindergarten or a new game he wanted them to play with him.

By the time they returned home after work, little time remained for much of anything besides dinner and, if they were lucky, a quick walk on the beach before it got dark. Then it was early to bed to be ready for the next work day.

Victoria had to admit that one thing she really missed was having a television set. They weren't allowed in the house, another of Mimi's rules. She had proclaimed television watching a mind-numbing, total waste of time. And maybe it was. But Victoria had always enjoyed flopping on the couch for a couple of hours to unwind before going to sleep. And she missed watching some of her favorite shows.

Victoria quickly developed a whole new respect for working mothers and began to realize how lucky she was that Madeline was there to take care of Andy in the afternoons and prepare dinner. At least that aspect of living with Brad's mother was a bonus, and Victoria made it a point to tell her mother-in-law how helpful she was. Although any time she did it, Madeline looked at her oddly as if to say, "Well, of course I am."

Still, Victoria felt guilty for not helping out more around the house, not performing the typical household duties she'd been doing her entire life. But Madeline did everything for them while they were at work. Everything. Not that Victoria wasn't grateful. It was nice to be able to relax in the evenings, but she wanted to participate in household duties. She felt like a guest in what was supposed to her own home.

One Sunday afternoon, in a rare moment, Victoria found herself alone in the living room with her mother-in-law while Brad and Andy played whiffle ball on the beach. She had been wanting to bring up the subject of participating more in the running of the household with Brad's mother, but hadn't had the opportunity.

As usual, Madeline's hair and make-up were perfectly done, and she wore another of her coordinated lightweight tunic tops and fitted pants, this one in pale blue. Victoria liked to relax around the house in gym shorts and T-shirts, and always felt incredibly underdressed next to her mother-in-law. Today was no exception.

Victoria complimented Madeline on her outfit, which she could see pleased her.

"If you'd like to see the catalog where I buy my clothes, I'd be happy to show it to you," her mother-in-law offered. "They have the nicest clothing. Much nicer than you'll find in the stores around here."

The gesture caught Victoria by surprise. She quickly thanked her mother-in-law and said she would love to look through it, although she knew she wouldn't buy anything. Madeline's clothes were lovely for a woman her age, but they weren't Victoria's style at all. Still, she tried to appear enthusiastic because Brad's mother rarely made friendly offers to her like that, and she certainly wasn't going to rebuff it.

Perhaps that was the reason Madeline had turned her down twice when she'd invited her to go shopping with her. She bought all her clothing from the catalog. Her mother-in-law also turned them down every time they invited her to go out to dinner with them. In fact, other than an occasional trip to the grocery store and her early morning jogs, Victoria thought it would take a forklift to get Madeline out of the house for anything.

After a few minutes of chitchat about fashion, Victoria broached the subject that was on her mind.

"Madeline," she began, "I feel so bad that you do so much for us, cooking and cleaning and watching Andy. I want to do more to help out."

Her mother-in-law shook her head. "I don't mind. I'm used to it, and I like things done a certain way. I'd really prefer to do it myself. And you and Bradley are busy at work anyway. Don't worry about it."

"Well, that's nice of you, but you should be out enjoying yourself more, doing things with your friends, not just taking care of us."

The older woman stiffened slightly. "I have my running in the morning, and twice a month I play bridge with my bridge group."

"But is that enough? Wouldn't you enjoy more companionship outside the family? Like maybe joining a community group or taking a class?"

Madeline eyed her warily. "I'm just fine. I have plenty to keep me busy."

"Well, what about dating? A lot of women your age date. Wouldn't you like to meet someone?"

Madeline waved her hand dismissively. "No. I have absolutely no interest in that. I don't need a man around to take care of who doesn't appreciate anything I do for him. I'm done with that."

"But you're so youthful looking for your age. I'm sure there are a lot of men who would be interested in you. Wouldn't it be nice to have someone to go out to dinner with? Maybe to travel with?"

The older woman pressed her lips together and her eyebrows knitted together into a frown.

"I don't like to eat out. The food is terrible. And I have no interest in traveling. I grew up in Europe, and now I live on the beach. Why would I want to travel? There's nowhere I haven't been where I want to go."

"I don't know," Victoria said. "It's a big world out there."

"I don't like to fly. Planes are dangerous."

Victoria realized the conversation was going nowhere. Another idea came to her.

"Have you traveled around Florida? To the west coast, to South Florida? I've always wanted to go to the Keys."

"Oh, yes," her mother-in-law responded, rolling her eyes. "Bradley's father dragged me all over the state. He loved to go sail fishing, especially in the Keys. I have no desire to go back. They don't have good beaches down there. The beach I have here is the best one in the state."

She doesn't want to travel, she doesn't want to date, she doesn't want to take classes. Victoria tried to think of what else she could get her mother-in-law focused on—anything else—other than this house and their family.

Another idea popped into her head. "What about volunteer work?" Victoria suggested enthusiastically.

"There must be all kinds of worthwhile charities around here."

Madeline stared at her for a long moment, a shrewd look coming into her eyes.

"Are you trying to get rid of me, Victoria?"

"No—no, of course not," Victoria answered, stumbling over her words. "It's just, well, we're not going to be around forever. Grown children eventually move away. It would be good if you had more activities to spend your time on, maybe have a companion closer to—"

"My age?"

"Well, yes."

Madeline stood up. "I'm just fine, Victoria. Don't you worry about me. I can take care of myself."

With that, she walked out of the room.

Even after their talk, Victoria continued to ask her mother-in-law every night if she could pitch in and help with dinner. But Madeline always said that she'd rather do it herself. Sometimes Victoria was relieved because she was tired from work, but other times it bothered her. It almost felt like Brad's mother didn't want her in the kitchen. It was as if it were her kitchen, and her kitchen alone. Victoria wasn't welcome there and that had really begun to upset her. If she was going to live here with her husband, she had to feel comfortable cooking in the kitchen.

Madeline was being nice enough, and Victoria could tell that, in her own way, she was making an effort. Especially when Brad was around. But there was a definite distance between them, as well as some tension, and her mother-in-law didn't direct a lot of conversation Victoria's way. Most of what she had to say was to Brad or Andy. If it was just the two of them, she basically ignored Victoria.

And Victoria often took offense at her mother-in-law's bossy nature, though she rarely spoke up about it. Madeline never hesitated to correct their table manners. It was constant with Andy, had grown more commonplace with Brad the longer they were there, and now she was even starting to do it to Victoria. Victoria found herself gnashing her teeth or literally biting down on her tongue to keep from saying something when Madeline reminded her not to put her elbows on the table, or that it was rude to bring her cell phone to the dinner table. It had been on the tip of her tongue several times to tell her mother-in-law that people who truly had good etiquette didn't correct other people's manners. But wanting to keep the peace, she kept the thought to herself, although it was getting more and more difficult for her to keep quiet.

And then there were the grammar corrections that Victoria had a particularly hard time accepting, especially from someone whose native language wasn't even English. But apparently when Madeline was growing up in Austria, and later when she moved to America, she had taken rigid coursework in English grammar. She complained regularly about how Americans butchered their own language and most didn't even know the basic rules of grammar. Victoria realized that was probably true, but it was still hard to take. Nobody likes to have their grammar corrected.

One night after dinner when Victoria said she was tired and was going to go "lay" down, Madeline reminded her that it was "lie" down, and then proceeded to give all three of them a five-minute mini-lecture about the difference. Visibly irritated, Victoria told her mother-in-law that she knew the rule but just didn't always use it in casual conversation. That was a mistake. Victoria then had to endure another lecture about how important it was to use correct grammar as a good example for the child. In the middle of it, Victoria shoved her chair back and excused herself from the table, telling everyone with emphasis that she was tired and was going to "lie" down.

Brad seemed numb to his mother's heavy-handed bossiness. It was as if he knew arguing would do no good and just automatically did what his mother told him to do. Maybe it wasn't that important to him, or maybe he was just so used to it that he didn't notice anymore. But his reactions seemed almost robotic, as if he zoned out and just did whatever was easiest to keep the peace.

For Victoria, though, as the days went on, she found herself wishing more and more that she could just eat dinner in her room to avoid all the unwanted "lessons." She could feel the anger and resentment rising, and she knew it wouldn't be long before it boiled over.

Chapter Fourteen

The dinners her mother-in-law cooked were always very healthy, full of lean meats, natural grains, and vegetables. Not that Victoria didn't eat healthy, but she was used to a little more variety in her food—and a lot more flavor. She knew her diet wasn't always the best, that she craved sweets, adored Mexican food, and wasn't adverse to a French fry or two. But she'd always eaten a lot of fruits and vegetables and tried to avoid fried foods and carb-laden prepackaged snacks as much as she could.

Victoria had been wanting to cook an authentic Italian dinner for Brad ever since they arrived, and she finally announced at Friday dinner that she'd like to prepare a special meal for them on Saturday night. Brad was enthusiastic about the idea, but Madeline didn't respond, and Victoria could see by her expression that she wasn't in favor of it.

But Victoria had been looking forward to preparing an Italian meal for Brad, and she was determined to do it. Excited, she pulled out all of her mother's favorite recipes, studied them for a couple of hours, and finally decided on her menu. It would be bruschetta for an appetizer, an antipasto salad, and Italian shells for the main course. And for dessert, cannoli, the cream-filled Italian pastry.

On Saturday morning, she went to a home goods store and spent an hour buying some special items for her table setting. Then, she spent the rest of the morning at a huge supermarket in Ponte Vedra buying all the ingredients. She was having a wonderful time shopping—this had to be the nicest grocery where she'd ever shopped. The grocery stores in California tended to be much more cramped and crowded and didn't have as much selection.

From the list she'd written the night before, Victoria bought all of her mother's special spices, eggs, semolina flour, and other ingredients to make the pasta, as well as tomatoes, artichokes, red peppers, romaine lettuce, genoa salami, and several different kinds of cheeses, including ricotta, mozzarella and parmesan. She also decided to bake the bread to be used both for the bruschetta and the garlic bread. Her cart was overflowing when she checked out, and she figured she spent over half a week's pay on all of the ingredients.

She had the best time making everything from scratch. When Andy occasionally popped his head in the kitchen, she'd grab him to help her pound the flour dough or stir the meat sauce. Brad peeked in occasionally, but she quickly shooed him away. Out of the corner of her eye, she caught sight of Madeline curiously surveying her kitchen, so soon afterward, she pulled the kitchen door shut to keep all the prying eyes out.

She was making a mess—a huge mess—and she knew it. But that was the way her mother had cooked, and that was the way she cooked. She would clean it all up when she was done, and the kitchen would look as good as new.

Finally, the dinner hour arrived. Victoria had gone a little over the top with her chef's outfit. She bought a black-and-white striped shirt and tied a red scarf around the top of her black pants like a cummerbund. She added another red scarf around her neck and a flat straw hat with a checkered band around it. She looked like she'd just fallen off a Venetian gondola.

Brad had dressed up for the evening too and was wearing a blue blazer and cream colored pants. Even Andy wore a little blue blazer with a pair of khaki pants. Only Madeline hadn't dressed for dinner, not even as much as she usually did. She wore a plaid shirtsleeve top and black pants.

Victoria went all Italian on the table setting too. She'd bought a small, four-piece set of bright red dinnerware that she set on a white tablecloth with red and white checkered napkins. A huge bowl of sunflowers served as the centerpiece. Apothecary jars filled with different kinds of dried pasta and dainty bottles of olive oil and balsamic vinegar were placed strategically around the table for decoration. Dean Martin songs filled the air.

Brad gushed with praise, both for her outfit and the table setting, and her mother-in-law even complimented the sunflowers. Andy giggled at her outfit, especially her hat.

Victoria had timed all the courses perfectly. When Brad, Madeline, and Andy were seated, she served the bruschetta and her favorite Italian red wine to the adults, and a raspberry sparkle fruit drink to Andy.

Brad rubbed his hands together in anticipation. "It smells great! I'm so hungry."

He reached for a piece of the toasted Italian bread buried in cheese and tomatoes and took a bite.

"Oh my God." He closed his eyes as he savored the flavors. "That's so delicious!"

Victoria flushed with pleasure. It meant everything to her that Brad thought she was a good cook and appreciated a good Italian meal. Andy tried a little piece, but his grandmother declined. Victoria took a bite and was thrilled at how tasty the bruschetta had turned out.

Andy drank the rest of the sweet raspberry sparkle drink with his straw, slurping to get the last remnants in the bottom of the glass.

"Yummy," he said with a big smile, handing his glass to Victoria. "Can I have another one?"

"Sure," Victoria answered at the same time her mother-in-law said with finality, "Absolutely not."

Then Madeline rebuked him. "Don't slurp, Andrew. You know better than that. And you may not have another one of those drinks. I'm sure they're all sugar. Give him milk instead."

Not sure what to say, Victoria turned to Brad.

Andy looked up at his father. "Can't I have another one, Daddy? The sparkler drink Mommy made is so good."

Brad was merrily enjoying his second piece of bruschetta when he stopped mid-bite, realizing that everyone at the table was staring at him. He became immediately uncomfortable.

"Uh, well, since this is a special occasion, with Victoria's first big dinner and all, I don't see why—" He stopped talking when he glanced at his mother, who was sending him a hard cold glare.

He hesitated. "Then again, that was an awfully big glass. If he has too much sugar, he'll be awake half the night. Maybe a glass of milk would be better, honey."

Victoria glanced at her mother-in-law to see a smile beginning to work at the corners of her lips. Irritated, Victoria decided not let Brad's siding with his mother bother her too much during her special dinner. They were probably right about the sugar, she told herself. She should have thought about that.

"Okay," she said. "Sorry, Andy, milk it is. Be right back."

While Andy pouted, Victoria went into the kitchen to get him a glass of milk, and also brought the second course to the table, the antipasto.

"What do we have now?" Brad asked eagerly when he saw the white platter.

"This is antipasto. My mother's favorite," she answered. "It's an Italian-style salad with genoa salami, pepperoni, artichokes and all kinds of other goodies. I hope you like it."

Brad scooped two heaping spoonfuls into his salad bowl, and forked a small amount for Andy. Brad's mother picked at the salad, separating out the vegetables and leaving the meats behind.

"This is great," Brad told Victoria. "I love the dressing."

His mother took a taste and screwed up her mouth as if she'd bitten into a lemon.

"There's so much garlic in it," she said, grimacing as she reached for a drink of water.

"That's what makes the recipe special," Victoria said, determined to ignore her mother-in-law's critical comment. "In my family, it was always the spicier, the better. I actually toned this down."

"Well, I love it, sweetheart," Brad said, raising his wine glass to her.

"The vegetables in it are tasty," Madeline said, obviously searching for some sort of compliment to give. "I just don't usually eat food this spicy."

"It's too picy for me too," Andy said, putting his fork down and looking at Victoria. "I don't like it."

He must have seen the disappointment on her face because he added, "I'm sorry, Mommy."

"Try some more, Andy," Brad began.

"No, Brad. It's okay. It probably is too spicy for him." Victoria couldn't help feeling a little upset that half the table didn't like her antipasto. "But you like it, right, Brad?"

"I love it! Best salad I ever had."

That made Victoria feel better. A lot better. After all, Brad was the one she was really cooking the dinner for, the one she wanted to please.

Next came the main course, stuffed shells that oozed three different kinds of cheese, baked sausage, and ground beef, smothered in tomato sauce and mushrooms.

Brad was the first to taste it. "Oh my God! This is the best food I've ever put in my mouth!"

Victoria could help but smile. He'd just made her day. But she noticed a hurt expression pass across her mother-in-law's face at Brad's comment, though she quickly tried to hide it. Victoria realized that after all the meals she'd cooked for her son, it couldn't have felt good to hear him say that.

"I like it too, Mommy," Andy said enthusiastically. "It tastes like pizza!"

Madeline took a small piece and forked through it, making a show of just taking a few small bites. Then she put her fork down and sat sipping her wine. When Victoria caught her eye, her mother-in-law gave her a pained half smile and said nothing.

Why do I care so much what she thinks? Victoria wondered. This meal is for Brad, not for her. Her first meal for her new husband. Victoria didn't think it would have mattered what she cooked. Her mother-in-law would have found something wrong with it. Trying not to get upset, she rebuked herself. Stop being so sensitive. Madeline's a health nut. She probably never eats Italian.

Victoria glanced at her mother-in-law. She was leaning back in her chair, the wine glass in her hand, staring blankly at the casserole dish holding the shells, a strange, subdued glare in her eyes. Victoria suddenly realized she was jealous. Brad hurt her feelings with the comment he made about the shells being the best food he's ever tasted, and she's jealous.

It didn't help when Brad and Andy both made grand gestures of wanting seconds. They were both being so sweet, trying to make her feel good. Such good manners. Like father, like son. Any other time she would have been thrilled by their attention. But not now. Their sweet intentions were only throwing gasoline on the flames.

Chapter Fifteen

Victoria entered the dining room holding four small dessert plates.

"And now, for the pîece de resistance!" she announced as she circled the table, depositing one small plate in front of each of them holding a tube-like shell with a white filling. "Cannoli—it's kind of like Italian ice cream, Andy!"

"Yay! Ice cream!" Andy clapped his hands.

"Now, Andy, it's Italian ice cream, so it tastes a little different," Victoria told him.

"I like it. It tastes good," Andy said, picking it up and eating it like a hot dog.

In an aside to Brad, she said, "It's actually a pastry filled with ricotta cheese, vanilla extract, and powdered sugar. But I thought he'd like it more if I said it was ice cream."

"It tastes wonderful, Victoria," Brad said. "A perfect, light dessert."

"More cheese," his mother said, setting down her fork in disgust. "I'm just going to have a cup of coffee."

Madeline stood up and walked toward the kitchen door. Panicked, Victoria called out to her, "No, no, Madeline. Please, don't go in there."

But it was too late. Her mother-in-law had already pulled open the kitchen door. The next moment, there was an ear-piercing scream.

"What is it, Mother?" Brad jumped up and rushed to the kitchen.

"Oh, God," Victoria cried, throwing down her napkin and pushing back her chair. "I didn't want anyone in the kitchen until I had time to clean up."

When they entered the kitchen, Brad's mother was leaning against the wall with her hand covering her mouth.

"Look at this! Look at this mess in my kitchen!" She fell into Brad's arms. Victoria wondered if she had fainted.

The kitchen did look like the aftermath of a small battle. Victoria knew that and planned to clean it up thoroughly after dinner. She'd used almost every pan hanging from the rack over the island, and most of them were coated with tomato sauce. Flour was spilled across the countertops, totally whiting it out in some places, and the remains of chopped vegetables covered the island. The sink overflowed with unwashed bowls, plastic containers, and cooking utensils. The tomato sauce that had boiled over on the stove had dripped down the side of the oven and spotted the floor below it.

"Don't worry about it, Madeline. I'll clean it up. I'm a sloppy cook, but I'm also a very good cleaner."

Madeline gave her a long, hard stare. Victoria felt as if those cold blue eyes were searing a hole into her.

"You'll never get this clean. My kitchen has never been this filthy."

Victoria approached her mother-in-law and put her arm around her shoulder. "Madeline, I'll take care of it. I promise. This is just the way we cooked in my house when I was growing up. Everything cleans up fine."

Madeline shook her off. "I cannot understand how anybody could be this dirty. It's disgusting. You should clean as you cook. It's so disrespectful to make such a mess in someone else's kitchen."

Victoria stiffened, and she could feel the anger rising. She tried to silence the thoughts that she wished she had the nerve to say. *Well, maybe that's the problem. I shouldn't be cooking in someone else's kitchen. I'm a married woman, and I should be cooking my own kitchen!*

Victoria couldn't remember the last time she'd felt this angry. She had looked forward to cooking this dinner for Brad for weeks, and now his mother had spoiled it. And for what? A few dirty pots and pans?

She glared back at her mother-in-law, fuming, and the words spilled out. "Well, maybe it's time I had my own kitchen."

Her mother-in-law looked like an angry lioness, ready to spring across the room at her prey.

Brad jumped in between them, raising his arms. "Now, now. C'mon. Calm down. Both of you. We've had a really nice dinner tonight. Let's not get upset over a few dirty dishes and say things we don't mean."

"Mommy?"

"What?!" Both Madeline and Victoria shouted, turning toward Andy at the same time.

Taken aback, Andy glanced back and forth between them, as if he didn't know what to say. Then he focused on Victoria.

"Mommy, I can help you clean up. I'm a good cleaner-upper."

Brad's mother turned her head away. She seemed hurt. "I thought he said Mimi."

"Thank you for offering, Andy, but I can clean it up all by myself. You can help another time," Victoria said.

She stared straight into her mother-in-law's crucifying eyes and added, "And it will be as sparkling clean as it was before this dinner."

"I'll believe that when I see it," Madeline hissed at her. She turned around sharply and rushed out of the room. Then she hurried up the upstairs.

Victoria felt shaken, and she could feel her eyes beginning to mist. This dinner had been so important to her, all the food had come out so well, and now it was ruined because of her mother-in-law. And for no good reason.

She felt a little hand slip into hers, pulling her down. Andy whispered in her ear, as if it were a secret. "I forgot to tell you. Mimi doesn't like messes. It makes her real mad."

141

"I can see that, Andy."

Brad put his arm around her shoulder. "Don't worry about it, Victoria. Mother is just extremely particular about her things. You'll get used to it."

Victoria felt like pushing him away and screaming at him. Instead, because Andy was there, she tried to control her emotions. In a hoarse whisper, she almost hissed at him, "Don't you get it, Brad? I don't want to 'Get used to it.' I want to have my own house, my own kitchen. I don't want a mother-in-law standing over me, being critical of every move I make."

Brad didn't say anything at first. He didn't seem to know what to say.

"Honey, it was still a great dinner," he told her in a consoling voice. "The best meal I ever had."

Victoria softened a little, but she felt like bursting into tears. He just didn't seem to get it. He didn't understand how much his mother's words and actions had hurt her on this special night.

Andy peered up at her with a confused expression on his face.

"Mommy?"

"What, Andy?" Victoria asked, looking down at him, her face still flushed with anger.

142

"Can I finish my ice cream?"

It took Victoria more than two hours to clean up the kitchen, and it wasn't pleasant. By the time she was finished though, the room was sparkling and just as clean, if not cleaner, than it had been before she cooked dinner.

As Victoria cleaned, she seethed, which may have given her the adrenalin she needed to scrub hard enough to get the caked-on tomato sauce off the pots and pans. Brad peeked in once or twice, offering to help, but seemed relieved when she declined. The last time he approached her, she told him to go on up to bed, and not to wait up for her. She wasn't in the mood to have a conversation with him or his mother.

What she felt like doing was calling her friend Shelly back in San Diego. She needed someone to talk to, to vent to, about how her mother-in-law had made a shambles of her first dinner. She picked up her phone to call but, at the last moment, decided against it. Shelly had tried to talk her out of marrying Brad after such a short courtship, told her she "was out of her mind," and Victoria wasn't in the mood for any "I told you so's," which Shelly had a tendency to enjoy. No, Victoria would wait to call her friend on a good day, when she had some happy news to report.

After all the heavy cleaning, Victoria didn't feel tired at all. She was keyed up and wanted to wind down somehow. Usually she would do that by watching a little television but, of course, there was no television set in Madeline's house. Her favorite show, *Saturday Night Live,* would be on in a few minutes, and that made her feel even worse.

Collapsing on the downstairs couch, she looked around for something to read. All she could find was a lean cooking magazine and a coffee table book on hiking trails in Florida. Neither enticed her in the least.

She noticed the Jacksonville newspaper in the magazine stand and picked it up. As she flipped through it, an advertising insert fell out from the department store where they had received the $500 gift certificate from their co-workers. Thumbing through it, she came across a forty-six-inch flat screen television set on sale that they could afford with the gift certificate. She would show this to Brad tomorrow. With everything she had to put up with living in this house, the least she could have was a TV set.

She read the rest of the paper, realizing how out of touch she had become with the rest of world during the past weeks. A television would also help her to keep up with the news, she decided.

She tossed the newspaper onto the coffee table, stood up, and stretched. But she still wasn't tired. Walking across the living room, she stopped at the sliding glass door and peered outside. The full moon lit up the patio, and a soft wind blew the sea oats in the distance. Unlocking the door, she stepped out onto the patio, ambled around the pool, and stood at the gate, gazing out at the moonlit beach and listening to the waves crash against the shore. She inhaled the moist sea air and basked in the soft touch of the salty air against her skin.

The cool ocean air felt refreshing until she realized goose bumps had begun to appear on her arms and then across her entire body. Something was off, and it was giving her chills. She had a feeling that she wasn't alone. A sixth sense told her that someone was watching her. Her body tensed, and she squinted out into the darkness. Scanning the patio, she slowly turned around toward the house. Then she saw her, saw her silhouette, standing in the window staring down at her. Her mother-in-law didn't move away from the window, didn't wave, but just stood and stared down at Victoria. Victoria held her gaze for what seemed like at least a minute. Then, finally, the drape slid across the window, and her mother-in-law was gone.

It took several hours for Victoria to fall asleep that night. She tossed and turned so much that she thought she surely would wake up Brad. But his steady, heavy breathing continued peacefully, and he slept through it all. She went over and over in her mind the high points and the horrible low point of the dinner. The shopping, the cooking, the serving—everything about the meal had been so enjoyable. Except for anything that had to do with Brad's mother. From her insinuations that the food was too fattening, to rebuking Andy at the table, to the hissy fit she threw when she saw the kitchen, Madeline couldn't have been more unpleasant. Didn't she realize what a special meal it was to Victoria? Or did she realize it and just not care? Or worse, was she so jealous that she purposely tried to sabotage it?

And then that long cold stare from the window. It made her shudder to even think about it.

Chapter Sixteen

It was late when Victoria awoke the next morning, nearly ten o'clock. When she went downstairs, she peeked through the blind and saw Brad sitting out on the patio, reading the newspaper. Andy was splashing around in the pool.

She wondered where Madeline was. Hopefully out for her morning run. She did *not* want to run into that woman today. As quietly as she could, she tiptoed to the kitchen and pulled the door open an inch. All clear.

Hurriedly, she poured herself a cup of coffee and grabbed a container of yogurt from the refrigerator. Glancing around the kitchen, she noticed several canisters and jars on the counter had been moved from the position where Victoria had left them last night, and some of the pots and pans had been rearranged on the hanging rack above the island. Obviously, her mother-in-law had made an inspection of her precious kitchen this morning and replaced everything to its proper order. She just had to let Victoria know that her cleaning job was not up to Madeline standards.

Stepping out onto the patio, carefully balancing her coffee cup, Victoria was surprised and delighted to be greeted by applause from Brad and Andy. It seemed a little rehearsed, but Victoria couldn't have appreciated it more.

"Kudos to the chef!" Brad said, jumping up to give her a kiss on the cheek.

"Hooray for the best cook in the whole wide world," Andy yelled, spraying water as he clapped his hands across the surface of the pool.

Her boys certainly knew how to make her feel good.

"Thank you very much," she said, setting her coffee cup down and taking a little bow. "It was my pleasure."

She sat down in the lounge chair next to Brad and watched Andy as he showed off his handstand and backward somersault. Both could use some work, but he was so proud of himself. Victoria gave him a hand.

"Mimi says my legs need to be straighter. Were my legs straight enough?"

"Your legs were just fine," Victoria answered. It took every ounce of energy she had to keep from rolling her eyes.

"So, what do you feel like doing today?" Brad asked her. "Any ideas?"

"As a matter of fact, I do have an idea of something I'd really like to do."

"You do?" Brad said, turning to her with interest. "And what's that?"

"Well, you know that $500 gift certificate the office gave us as a wedding gift?"

Brad raised an eyebrow. "I believe I remember something about that." He grinned at her. "I figured it had been burning a hole in your pocket."

"I know it's for both of us, but what I'd really like to buy with it is a television set. I miss my TV. And they're having a sale on them at the store."

Andy let out a whoop. "Yes! Yes! A TV set. All the other kids have one and they get to watch SpongeBob and Fireman Sam and Spider-Man. Please, please, please, Daddy, can we get a TV set?"

"Okay, okay. It sounds like I'm outnumbered. I know you like to watch TV, Victoria, and Andy's been asking for one for a while. And actually, I'd like to watch some golf and baseball too."

Andy was beside himself with excitement.

"Now, Andy," his father told him, "if we get a TV, there will be limits on how much you're allowed to watch. No more than an hour a day."

Andy nodded his head, and kept nodding it for at least three seconds. "I will. I promise. An hour of TV is better than no hours of TV."

Brad's face suddenly took on a pensive tone, his eyebrow squeezed together, and he made the slightest of grimaces.

"You're thinking about your mother, aren't you? About what she's going to say."

He looked at her in surprise and nodded. "She's not going to like it, but it's time she joined the twenty-first century. If my bride wants a TV set, she's going to get a TV set."

Andy came dripping out of the pool. "I want to come along. I want to go to the TV store."

"Sure, Andy, you can come," his father told him, as he wrapped a towel around him and started drying him off. "But you have to be on your good behavior in the store."

"Don't worry, Daddy. I will!"

When Andy was dry enough to go in the house, the three of them raced upstairs to get dressed and then took off for Jacksonville to spend their gift certificate. Victoria didn't see Brad's mother before they left, but thought she heard her come in from running. Brad hollered up that they were going shopping and were taking Andy with them, but received no response.

When they reached the store, the television set was discounted even more than they expected, leaving over fifty dollars for them to spend on something else. Not seeing anything else in the appliance department that interested them, they wandered over to sporting goods. Brad started trying out some putters, while Andy and Victoria roamed through the other aisles, looking at the tennis rackets and camping equipment.

At the edge of the department were dozens of bicycles, in all shapes and sizes, from tricycles for toddlers to ten-speeds for adults. Victoria hadn't seen a bicycle around the house, so she guessed that maybe Andy didn't have one yet. A few of the bikes looked just about the right size for him, and she noticed they were on sale too. Buying a bike for Andy would be a great use of the rest of the gift card.

"Hey, Andy, come look at the bicycles. What do you think?"

Andy was standing away from the bicycles, leaning away from them with his back pushed up against a shelf of sleeping bags. Standing still as a statue, a worried frown contorted his sweet little face. He appeared to be frozen in fear.

"Andy? What's the matter? Don't you like bicycles?"

The odd paralyzing expression didn't leave his face. He shook his head and then stared down at his feet, not saying anything.

"Andy? What's the matter?"

She walked over to him, knelt down, and put her index finger under his chin, lifting his face to hers. She didn't know if his expression was one of sadness or fear. Or maybe both.

"Tell me what's wrong, Andy."

He shook his head again, staring at her with a blank expression of fear.

"You can tell me, Andy. I'm your mommy. You can tell me anything."

Tears welled in his eyes and, in a voice barely louder than a whisper, he said, "My other mommy got runned over when she was riding her bike."

Victoria gasped and covered her mouth with her hand. "Oh no!"

She had no idea that's how Andy's mother had died. No wonder the bicycle department traumatized him. It would have been nice if someone had told her so she could have avoided upsetting the poor child! She took hold of his hand and walked him out of the department as fast as she could. Looking for a distraction, she noticed the sign up ahead.

"Let's go to the toy department!"

Still appearing shell-shocked, Andy nodded and they started walking quickly down the aisle. When he tugged on her hand, she knelt down to him.

"Mommy," he said, tears still welling in his eyes. "Promise me you won't ride a bicycle."

Victoria thought her heart would break. "I promise, Andy. I will never ride a bicycle."

She pulled him into a big bear hug and had to call on every ounce of self-control she possessed not to start crying herself.

When they reached the toy department, he began to perk up a little, and by the time they found the *Star Wars* toys and figurines, he was almost back to normal.

"Daddy took me to see *Star Wars*," he told her excitedly, grabbing a plastic R2D2 figure. "It's the best movie I ever saw!"

He pointed out every *Star Wars* figure that he knew, telling her their names, and the two of them fought some pretend battles with them.

Victoria kept looking up for Brad, wondering when he would figure out where they were and catch up with them.

When Brad finally did find them, he was carrying a golf putter.

"I had a feeling this was where you might be," he said with a laugh.

Andy ran to him, Darth Vader and Luke still in his hands. "Daddy, are you going to buy a golf club? Like the kind we played with at goofy golf?"

"Exactly that kind, Andy. Very good! Daddy likes to have his own putter to help him play better."

Brad turned to Victoria, who was putting the Star Wars figures Andy had pulled out back into their correct bins.

"Would you mind too much, honey, if I bought this putter with the rest of the money?"

Victoria shrugged and didn't look up. "Whatever."

Brad paused, obviously confused by her demeanor. "If you'd rather get something else, that's fine too. I just thought—"

"The golf club is fine, Brad," Victoria said, the irritation in her voice clear. "It's not about the golf club."

Brad scratched his head. "Am I missing something? I don't understand—"

"We'll talk about it when we get home." She turned away from him to Andy and softened her tone. "Andy, go ahead and pick out whichever *Star Wars* figure you want, and I'll buy it for you. Okay?"

Andy's eyes lit up. "Really?"

She nodded.

He quickly searched through the bin and pulled one out. "I want Chewbacca."

"Chewy is my favorite too," Brad told him, obviously trying to lighten the mood. He gave his son a high five.

Victoria ignored him and walked ahead to the register.

Chapter Seventeen

They had driven half way home before Victoria calmed down. If she was going to be a good mother to Andy, there were things she needed to know, and either Brad or his mother should have told her about this. She had traumatized the poor child unnecessarily. Andy was so upset. She would be having a long talk with Brad tonight.

Victoria took a deep breath and tried to push the incident to the back of her brain so the day wouldn't be spoiled. She reached over and squeezed Brad's hand. The look he gave her was filled with so much relief that she immediately felt guilty. This was one of their first real fights, and poor Brad didn't even know what they were fighting about. Maybe it was just too painful for him to talk about his wife's accident, and here she was blaming him for not telling her about it. Still, for Andy's sake—

When they pulled into the driveway, Brad popped open the back of the SUV and pulled out the big cardboard box containing the flat screen TV. Victoria asked him if she could help him carry it, but he told her he could handle it by himself.

He took it into the foyer and set it on the floor.

"Where do you think we should put it?" he asked, glancing around.

Before Victoria could respond, Madeline came around the corner from the kitchen.

"Put what?" she asked, eyeing the box.

All three of them stood silently staring at her. No one wanted to tell her about their purchase.

Madeline cocked her head sideways and squinted her eyes. It seemed to take her a minute to figure out the contents.

"Flat screen?" She looked closer, and then it registered. She pursed her lips into a firm line.

She gave Brad a disappointed look and said simply, "Why?"

He fidgeted a bit before answering. Visibly nervous, he started one of his long-winded explanations. "Well,

Mother, the folks at work gave us a five hundred dollar gift certificate for a wedding gift. Victoria thought a television would be the perfect purchase. She had to leave hers in California and likes to unwind watching it after work. And I wouldn't mind watching some sports and, of course, the news. I don't want Andy to feel out of place at school where all the other children have television sets. We'll limit his watching and only let him watch approved shows and—"

"Ok, Brad. That's enough," Victoria said, taking hold of his arm. "Madeline, we wanted a television set, and we bought one. Now, the only question is, where will we put it."

Brad inhaled audibly at her comment and slowly released the air. Unsmiling, Madeline's stony blue eyes fixed onto her. Victoria met her gaze. No one said anything.

"How about in the living room?" Brad said finally. "Over there, in the corner."

Everyone glanced at the corner of the living room, but no one said anything.

"No," Victoria said. "The point of having the television is to relax and unwind after work. Let's put it in the sitting area of the master suite. That way, we won't bother your mother while we're watching it."

Madeline shrugged and turned to leave. "If you're determined to rot your brains, put it wherever you want."

Victoria pressed her lips together and rolled her eyes. "C'mon. Let's get this thing set up."

As Brad carried it upstairs, Victoria reminded him, "You know we're going to have to get cable too, don't you? We'll only get a few stations without it."

Brad shrugged. "So, we'll get cable."

"That means technicians coming out to the house, holes being drilled for their wires, the whole bit. Your mother isn't going to like it."

He thought for a second and then shrugged. "She'll just have to get used to it. It is the twenty-first century after all."

It didn't take long for Brad to get the television set up and running. Andy watched his every move, and Brad deemed him his "apprentice." Andy cheered when the first picture appeared on the screen. Brad flipped around to the few network stations they could get without cable, hoping to find something Andy might like to watch. The television included a built-in DVD player, but they didn't have any movies. Finding no children's shows on Sunday afternoon, Brad turned on a golf tournament, and Andy climbed onto his lap to watch it with him.

Madeline didn't cook on Sundays, and begged off again when they asked her if she wanted to go out to dinner with them at a nearby oyster bar. The restaurant was a typical beach dining establishment, a ramshackle shack with blue awnings and tall stools crowded around a long wooden bar. It was crammed with sunbathers grabbing a bite to eat in the waning light of the afternoon before heading home from the beach. They found three stools, and Victoria definitely broke her diet as the three of them chowed down on baskets full of fried shrimp, French fries, and cole slaw. Feeling rebellious after her television purchase, Victoria was tempted to order a Coke too, but changed her mind at the last minute and got a lemonade. No need to start a full on mutiny!

By the time they returned home, it was bedtime for Andy and talk time for Victoria and Brad. The minute they were alone in their bedroom, she took him by the hand and led him to the two armchairs in the sitting room.

"We need to talk."

The color drained from Brad's face at the words most men dread hearing.

"Talk? That doesn't sound good."

Victoria nodded and paused before beginning. "Brad, I know we made a pact not to talk about our past relationships. And we've both respected that. But if there is information I need to know in my role as stepmother to Andy, you have to tell me."

"Information? I don't understand."

"There was an incident today at the store that hurt Andy that could have been totally avoided if you had been more candid with me."

"Hurt?" Brad said, suddenly alarmed. "What happened to Andy?"

"He's fine now," she assured him. "But, Brad, I took him into the bicycle department and asked him why he didn't have a bike."

Brad's face froze. "Oh God."

"He had a terrible reaction."

"Oh no. What happened?"

"Well, he got very upset and started to cry. He seemed traumatized by it for about ten minutes afterward."

Brad leaned forward and put his head in hands.

"You should have told me, Brad. You should have told me how your wife died."

Brad jerked his head up, surprised.

"How do you know about that?' he asked suspiciously. "What do you know about it? Who told you?"

Victoria was taken aback by his tone. "I know," she said, "because Andy told me when I asked him why he was so upset about the bicycles."

Brad closed his eyes and groaned. "I'm sorry that happened," he said. "I didn't even think about there being bicycles in that store. Andy is terrified of bicycles. I always try to distract him when I see someone riding one along the road."

"I just wish you had confided in me. Don't you understand that's something I needed to know?"

He reached over and took hold of her hands. "Yes, yes, of course. I didn't think about that, and I should have. I'm sorry."

Neither of them said anything for several moments. Victoria hesitated to ask for information, but now that the subject was out there, she wanted to know more.

"What happened to your wife? I guess I just assumed she died of an illness, and I didn't want to ask you about it, you know, because of the pact. I didn't want to upset you. Andy said she was run over while she was riding her bike?"

"You know, I don't even know how Andy knows that's how she died. I didn't tell him. Mother must have. Or he probably overheard us talking."

Victoria pushed ahead. Was he avoiding her question?

"But what happened to her, Brad?"

Brad swallowed hard and ran his hand through his hair.

"Erica liked to take long bike rides. The only place to really ride out here is along A1A. As you've probably noticed, it's not that wide. I told her it was dangerous, but she just laughed it off."

He paused, and she wasn't sure if he was going to continue.

"When was she hit?" Victoria asked.

"On a Monday morning. A hit-and-run. They never found out who ran over her. She was hit so hard that her body was thrown about thirty feet off the road into some bushes."

Victoria gasped. "That's so horrible."

He hung his head. "Devastating. It's not something I like to talk about."

Victoria reached over and touched his arm. "I'm so sorry, Brad."

He nodded, continuing to stare down at the floor.

"Where were you? How did you find out?"

"I was at work. The police came to the office in the afternoon. They found out who she was by the registration tag on her bike. It took them a while to find me."

"And they never found out who ran over her?"

Brad shook his head. "They investigated for quite a while, but nothing ever turned up. They weren't even actually sure when it happened. When I left for work, she was still in bed, so I don't even know what time she went out riding. They said it looked like her body had been in the brush for a few hours."

"Oh God. The poor woman. Who found her?"

"Another cyclist who rode by and saw the mangled bike."

"I'm so sorry, Brad," she said, reaching out to hold his hand.

They sat silently for several moments. Victoria suddenly felt guilty for feeling angry with Brad. What a sad burden he had been carrying.

She didn't want to put him through anymore heartache, so she tried to think of a more pleasant subject.

"Hey," she said. "There's one leftover cannoli in the fridge. Race ya for it!"

Relief filled his face, but she only saw it for a second. Then he was out the door, racing down the stairs.

Chapter Eighteen

Victoria loved her new job. Maybe it was having her own office, maybe it was knowing that Brad was right down the hall, but she already felt more content here than she ever did in San Diego.

And she was making a new friend, Kate, from the office next door. They chatted over coffee every morning and had gone to lunch together twice. She learned that Kate was married, too, and had a six-year-old daughter, Sara. They were already talking about getting together for a play date with their children, and maybe double dating as a couple.

Victoria had a busy Monday morning and groaned when she realized she needed to make multiple copies of a proposal she had just finished. As she stood in the copy room tapping her fingers on the machine, willing it to move faster, the unfriendly woman she'd met the first day entered the copy room holding some correspondence on letterhead stationery. The tanned woman with the short black hair was tiny, much smaller than Victoria. Victoria had never spoken to her because the woman avoided eye contact every time they passed each other in the hall. But Victoria was determined to make an effort.

"Hello," Victoria said, extending her hand. "I'm Victoria Reynolds. I know we met, but I'm sorry, I don't remember your name. Everything was such a blur that first day."

The smaller woman glanced at her hand and seemed to be deciding whether she would shake it or not. After a longer-than-comfortable pause, she extended her hand and shook Victoria's. But she didn't say anything.

"Please forgive me, but what is your name again?" Victoria asked.

Again a long pause. Was she going to answer? Victoria wondered.

"Lana. I'm Lana."

"It's nice to meet you, Lana. I won't be too much longer. In fact, since you only have a couple of pages, I can stop and you can go ahead if you'd like."

Lana shrugged and shook her head. "I'm in no rush. Go ahead and finish."

There was an uncomfortable silence, and Victoria busied herself more than she needed to, straightening the copies that had already come out of the machine.

"So," the voice came from behind her. "How are you getting along with the dragon lady?"

Did she hear her right? She turned around to face her co-worker. "Excuse me?"

"I asked you how you were getting along with the dragon lady." Lana's tone was unexpectedly direct.

Victoria knew immediately who she was talking about, but she wasn't going to denigrate her, admittedly, less-than-perfect mother-in-law to an employee at her husband's workplace.

"I'm sorry," Victoria replied innocently. "I don't know what you mean."

"Oh, come on. You know exactly who I mean." Victoria was surprised by the woman's aggressive tone.

"Not really. Could you explain it to me?" Victoria asked, in the same innocent tone.

"Your new mother-in-law, of course. There's no way that woman isn't getting under your skin."

Victoria wasn't sure what to say, but her curiosity got the best of her. "You know my mother-in-law?"

Lana gave a dismissive laugh. "Oh, I know Mrs. Reynolds. Too well. In fact, if it hadn't been for her," Lana said, glancing down at Victoria's hand, "I might be wearing that ring right now instead of you."

Instinctively, Victoria drew her left hand up to her chest and covered it with her other hand, as if she were protecting it from this aggressive woman.

"What?" she asked, wondering if she had heard the woman correctly.

"You heard me."

Victoria didn't know what to say, so she said nothing.

Lana continued. "That manipulative bitch did everything she knew how to break up Brad and me."

Victoria absorbed the information. So Brad had dated this woman. She wondered when, but couldn't bring herself to ask the question. She continued to stare at Lana, saying nothing.

When she heard no reply, Lana went on, "Brad's mom is a real piece of work. You'd think she was his wife, not his mother. Can't stand another woman getting more of his attention than she does."

Lana's words certainly had a ring of truth to them, but Victoria wouldn't give her the satisfaction of knowing that she agreed.

"You're talking about my mother-in-law," Victoria said in a tone of soft rebuke. "We're family now."

Lana ignored her comment and kept talking. "Of course, they say a man will treat his wife the way he treats his mother. So I guess you're lucky there. You probably have him jumping through hoops just like she does."

Victoria's temper started to flare. "I beg your pardon. I do not have my husband 'jumping through hoops.'"

Lana shrugged as if she didn't care. "Just be glad you met Brad when you were a few thousand miles away, or she would have sabotaged your relationship with him too. She'll stop at nothing."

The copy machine stopped vibrating, and Victoria turned her back on Lana, arranged all of her print outs, and gathered them together to return to her desk.

"Don't forget what I said," Lana warned her, as Victoria stepped out of the copy room. "She'll try to sabotage you. Watch your back."

The confrontation unsettled Victoria. The woman obviously didn't like her, so why was she giving her advice to try to help her? Could she believe what Lana said about Brad's mother? And when had she dated Brad—and for how long?

Brad was out of the office until late afternoon, but she would ask him about it later. Until then, though, she wanted a woman's perspective on the situation. She wanted to know more about Brad's relationship with this Lana woman. So she asked Kate if she was free for lunch.

Victoria didn't like airing the family's business at the office, but she trusted Kate not to say anything to anyone else. Over spinach salads, Victoria asked her if Brad and Lana had dated. Kate wasn't surprised by the question.

"I was wondering how long it would take for you to find out. I just didn't want to be the one to tell you. Didn't want it to cause any problems in the office."

"Oh no, of course not. I don't like office gossip either. It's just that she approached me in the copy room."

"She did?" Kate said, not able to hide her interest. "What did she say?"

Victoria took a sip of her iced tea before answering. "She warned me about Brad's mother. She said she sabotaged their relationship and if wasn't for her, she'd be wearing this ring now," Victoria said, automatically lifting her left hand to show Kate her ring.

"That's ridiculous," Kate said emphatically, rolling her eyes. "I mean, I don't know anything about the mother, but it was very obvious to everyone in the office that she was much more into Brad than he was into her."

"Really?" Victoria felt slightly relieved. "How long did they date?"

Kate twisted her lips and looked up at the ceiling. "I don't know exactly. Maybe two months? Not long. I know a few of the guys had an office pool going on how long it was going to last."

Victoria couldn't help chuckling. "That's embarrassing."

"Sure was," Kate said with a laugh. "She really went after him. Always stopping by his office. Asking him to go to lunch. Taking him little snacks. You know, that kind of thing. It was so obvious. Everyone thought Brad just took her out because he was lonely, or because he didn't want to hurt her feelings. You know how nice he is."

Victoria nodded. That sounded like Brad. "Well, when was this? When did they stop seeing each other?"

Kate thought for a moment. "Let's see. She was hanging all over him at the Christmas party, but I don't think it was too long after that. Maybe four or five months ago."

Victoria grimaced. That was pretty recent.

"No wonder she's still upset. I could tell the first day I met her that she didn't like me. She seemed to resent me."

Kate hesitated. She looked like she was going to say something, and then stopped.

"What?" Victoria asked, frowning.

"Well—"

"What? Tell me."

She could tell Kate didn't want to tell her, but her friend finally relented. "Okay. Lana had asked to have Dave's office when she found out he was retiring and was telling everybody that it would be hers. She had seniority in the office. But then—"

"I came along." Victoria sighed. "She must hate me. First I get Brad, and then I get her office."

"Well, that's not your fault. You deserved both, and you got both."

"Still."

Kate shrugged. "She'll get over it. What other choice does she have?"

Victoria considered the question and said to herself, "Hopefully not to make my life miserable."

Chapter Nineteen

On the drive home that night with Brad, Victoria brought up the subject of Lana.

He sighed and reddened a little. "I figured you'd hear about that sooner or later. But remember our pact."

"I know, I know. But it's kind of different when it's someone in the office."

"It was nothing. I promise." He glanced over at her from the steering wheel. "We didn't go out that long, and it's been over for months."

"I'm not upset," Victoria assured him. "It's just, she kind of cornered me today in the copy room and said some things about your mother."

She could tell that Brad didn't like that. At all. "What did she say about my mother?"

"Well, that your mother sabotaged your relationship with her. That she would probably be wearing this ring right now if it weren't for your mother."

"Hah! That's a laugh." She had never heard that bitter tone in his voice before.

"Well, what happened between her and your mother?"

Brad shrugged and seemed to be trying to remember. "Nothing in particular that I can remember. I could tell they didn't like each other from the first time they met. Mother said she was rude."

"She said your mother sabotaged your relationship."

"It wasn't a relationship," Brad said emphatically, glancing over at her with a serious look. "We just dated a little bit."

He thought for few moments. "Mother didn't want her to come over for Christmas. I remember that. She thought it should be just family for Andy's sake."

"That's understandable," Victoria said. "That's all?"

"Nothing else I can think of. Except I do remember Lana being upset when we couldn't go out on New Year's Eve. Mother got sick at the last minute, too late for me to find a babysitter, so I had to stay home with

Andy. I didn't like the way Lana acted when I had to cancel, and we didn't go out after that."

Hmmm. Victoria could see how Lana might think Madeline played sick on purpose to ruin their New Year's Eve date. She wouldn't put it past her mother-in-law to pull a trick like that.

When Victoria didn't respond, Brad said, "Do you want me to say something to Lana? I don't like her approaching you like that at work. You shouldn't have to deal with things like that."

"Oh no," Victoria assured him. "I'm sure she's still just a little jealous. And, then, I got the office she thought she was going to get. So, I guess I'm not her favorite person."

Brad glanced over at her and frowned. "What's this about your office?"

"Kate said Lana told everyone she was going to get the open office. And then I got it instead."

"Oops," Brad said, lifting his eyebrows. "I didn't know about that."

He thought for a moment. "But still, I may talk to her. I don't like her saying things about you and Mother around the office."

Victoria shook her head. "Don't this time. I can deal with it. If she says anything else, or if it seems like it's getting out of hand, I'll let you know."

He reached over, picked up her hand, and kissed it. "If that's what my bride wants, that's what we'll do."

Victoria smiled at him and rubbed the back of his hand with her thumb. They rode along in silence for a few minutes before Brad said, "Oh, I forgot to tell you. I just found out today, I have to go to Tampa for a couple of days for meetings. I'll drive down tomorrow night and won't be back until Friday."

Victoria cringed. That meant she would be alone in the house with Madeline, eating at the dinner table with just her and Andy. That did not sound like an attractive situation at all.

Brad noticed immediately. "What's the matter? Can't stand to be away from your groom for a couple of days?"

"Well, it will be the first time we've been apart since we met."

"You know, that's right. I hadn't thought about that."

"I wish I could go with you," she said. "What are these meetings about, anyway?"

Brad shrugged. "Using insurance as part of estate planning. We're looking at some different packages. Boring stuff. You know."

Victoria nodded. "I guess I am glad I'm not going."

"Oh," he said, as if he'd just thought of it. "Speaking of insurance, you and I need to update our life insurance plans."

"What do you mean, update? I don't have any life insurance."

Brad pretended to be aghast. "A soon-to-be financial planner who doesn't follow her own advice?"

"I didn't have anyone to protect, anyone to leave it to," she protested.

"Well, you do now," he said. "We both have Andy to protect. If anything happens to one of us, the other one will need to support him until he's old enough to support himself."

Victoria looked thoughtful. "I guess that's true. We're both so young, I hadn't thought about it that way."

Brad reached over and poked her in the side with his forefinger. "Hey, girl, if you're going to talk the talk, you've gotta walk the walk."

Victoria had never even considered life insurance for herself, although she'd often preached it to others. Brad was right.

"Okay. I'm convinced. How much do you think we should get on each other?"

"I'm thinking about two million each."

"Two million dollars!" Victoria was stunned.

"Well, think about it, babe. Andy's five. We're talking housing, clothing, food, educational expenses for the next fifteen years or so. That adds up. It's a whole new ballgame when there's a child involved."

Victoria lifted her eyebrows and quickly ran some numbers in her head.

"You know, when you add in everything, two million really isn't that farfetched."

Brad grinned at her. "And just think how less painful it will be for you when I kick off and you get a check for two million dollars."

She slapped his arm. "Don't even kid about that."

He laughed, but then said seriously, "It will make me feel better knowing that you and Andy are protected if anything should happen to me. I'll get it all set up while I'm in Tampa. I know a good life man."

Victoria nodded and suddenly felt very lucky. It was nice having someone looking out for her.

As she sat quietly staring out the window, the thought of Brad being out of town for two days began to depress her. After they'd driven a few miles in silence, he glanced over at her.

"What's wrong, honey? My kidding around about the life insurance didn't upset you, did it?"

She shook her head and said dismissively, "Oh no. That's not it."

"What then?"

"I shouldn't say?"

"Shouldn't say what?" he asked.

She wasn't sure if she should say anything. She didn't want Brad to worry while he was away on a business trip.

"Well," she began, "I just don't feel that comfortable with it being just your mother and me in the house after the dinner fiasco Saturday night. And then the TV thing—"

Brad interrupted. "Oh, don't worry. That'll smooth out. I'll talk to her again if you want me to."

"I don't know, Brad. Maybe. But can you at least wait to leave until after dinner tomorrow night?"

"Of course. I was thinking about doing that anyway. It's only a three-hour drive to Tampa."

"I really wish I could go with you."

"I do too. But that wouldn't go over too big at the office, would it?"

She shook her head. "I know."

If she and Madeline weren't getting along any better by the time Brad left, Victoria decided she might go out to dinner in Jacksonville after work, or maybe grab some takeout and eat it upstairs while she watched television. The thought of sitting across the dinner table from Madeline for two nights without Brad sounded like sheer torture to her.

She tried to get her mind off the prospect of Brad not being home and think of something more pleasant to talk about.

"Hey," she said, grabbing his sleeve with a grin. "Remember what day Sunday is?"

"How could I forget? My big day."

"What do you want to do for Father's Day?"

"Anything you'd like, my dear. You plan it."

It had been so long since Victoria had taken part in a Father's Day celebration that she didn't have a clue of what to do. Her father had died when she was in the first grade. She tried to imagine the scene from all the television commercials and magazine ads she'd seen.

"How about a barbeque on the patio and then a day on the beach? I can't get enough of watching you surf."

Brad gave her a broad smile. "A cookout and surfing sounds perfect. I can't think of anything I'd like more."

When they pulled into the driveway, Andy was perched on the front porch waiting for them, as usual, and a few minutes later dinner was on the table. Brad disappeared in the kitchen while Victoria entertained Andy, and she guessed he was speaking to his mother as he said he would.

At the dinner table, everything seemed to be back to normal to Victoria, if anything about this strange living arrangement could be called normal. During dinner, Madeline was as pleasant as she seemed capable of being, and nothing more was said about the flare-ups over the weekend.

Chapter Twenty

Brad left for Tampa Tuesday night after dinner as planned, and Victoria immediately excused herself and went upstairs to their suite. Exhausted from work, she changed into her nightgown and lay down on the couch in the sitting room to see if she could find something to watch on television. She turned off the lights, flipped around on the remote control, and settled on a sitcom that she'd never seen but had heard was supposed to be funny.

She must have dozed off in the semi-darkened room when she suddenly awoke with a start. A dark figure stood over her, staring down at her.

She screamed. "Who is it?" she called out, clutching her nightgown to her chest.

"Victoria. Are you asleep already?" a familiar voice asked in a coarse whisper.

"Oh, Madeline. You scared me to death."

Victoria leaned her arm back behind her head and turned on the lamp.

Madeline glanced toward the television and pressed her lips into a frown. Victoria quickly muted the set. She looked at her mother-in-law expectantly.

"Victoria, my dentist called and is able to fit me in tomorrow afternoon for an appointment. Could you pick up Andrew from school?"

Victoria tried to focus her brain. She was still half asleep.

"Uh, sure. I can take a late lunch and pick him up."

"Good. Just bring him home and wait with him until I get back. It shouldn't be too long."

"Okay, sure. Let's see. He gets off at 2 o'clock, right? And what's the address of his school."

Madeline mumbled something that she didn't hear.

"What?" Victoria asked. "I didn't hear you."

"I'll get the address." Her mother-in-law left the room and returned a minute later with a piece of notebook paper. She gave her the directions in far more detail than Victoria needed.

"Sure," Victoria said. "I'll be happy to pick him up."

"Thank you," Madeline said. She made a point of leaning forward and staring Victoria straight in the eye. "I'm counting on you."

Good grief, Victoria said to herself. Does she think I'm a moron? I think I can handle picking up a little boy from school.

After Madeline left, Victoria clicked off the television set and went to bed. It felt so strange to be alone in that big king-size bed all by herself. A sadness fell over her as she thought about this being their first night apart. She hoped there wouldn't be many. She couldn't wait for Brad to come home. She was surprised at how much she missed him.

She was incredibly busy the next day at work, but rearranged her day so she could leave at 1:20 p.m. to have plenty of time to drive to Andy's school. She'd never been there, so she was looking forward to seeing it.

She had munched on some Fritos from the vending machine for lunch and was just getting ready to leave the office when her cell phone rang.

"Why haven't you picked up Andrew?" the familiar female voice screamed at her. "You told me you would pick him up."

Victoria recognized her mother-in-law's voice immediately, but she was stunned by the call. "I—I'm just getting ready to leave work to go get him."

"Getting ready to leave! He gets off at 1 o'clock on Wednesdays."

"But I thought he got out of school at 2 o'clock?"

"Every day but Wednesday. I told you that last night."

Victoria was shocked at her mother-in-law's words. "No, you didn't. We discussed that he got out at 2 o'clock."

Madeline's voice was even sharper than usual. "That's ridiculous. We did not. Obviously, you can't be trusted to do anything."

Victoria hurriedly picked up her purse and keys. "I'm sorry. I'm leaving right now. I should be there in twenty-five minutes or so."

"Twenty-five minutes! I'm in the dentist chair. Do I need to get up and go get him? Andy is in tears." Madeline harsh voice sliced through the phone line.

"No, no. Stay where you are. I'm on my way!"

Victoria ran out of the office, jumped into her car, and headed for the highway to Andy's school. Traffic was backed up on the exit ramp to the beach road, and she had to sit through two red lights before she was able to make her turn. Her heart pounding, she found herself silently cursing slow drivers who were poking along, just out for a day at the beach. She used her horn to speed them up more than once.

When she was about halfway to the school, her cell phone rang again. This time, it was Brad.

"What's going on, Victoria? I just got a call from Andy's school, and he's nearly hysterical wondering where you are? Did you about forget him?"

Weaving to get into a faster lane, Victoria felt like throwing the phone out the window.

"No, I did NOT forget him! Your mother didn't tell me he got out of school an hour earlier on Wednesdays."

"She told me she did."

Victoria held the phone away from her ear and stared at it. Was Brad siding with his mother?

"Well, she didn't, Brad. Who do you believe, her or me?"

Brad paused. "That's not important. How far away are you? Andy's all by himself with only one secretary. And she didn't sound too happy. Everyone else is gone."

"I've never been there before, but I think I'm about five minutes away. Let him know I'm almost there."

"Okay," he said, clicking off.

She tried to calm herself down, but her heart was racing. She was absolutely positive that Madeline didn't tell her she needed to be there at 1 o'clock today. She would have remembered that.

She made a couple of wrong turns trying to find the school but finally arrived at 1:50, fifty minutes late. As Andy ran to the car, Victoria could see that his face was puffy and tear-stained. The secretary, dangling her car keys with a look of rebuke on her face, opened the door and strapped Andy in, uttering just one sentence before she slammed the door shut, "Everyone knows it's 1 o'clock on Wednesdays."

Andy peered up at her with his red-rimmed eyes, an expression of deep hurt on his face? "Did you forget about me?"

"Oh no, Andy. I would never forget about you. I didn't know that school got out early on Wednesdays."

"Mimi said you forgot about me."

Victoria felt her ire rise. How dare she?

"Well, Mimi is wrong. I thought you got out of school at 2 o'clock, just like you do every other day. I was leaving work early to be sure I got here on time."

Andy sniffled and looked up at her. "Everybody else was gone for a long time. I was all by myself."

"I know and I'm so sorry, Andy."

He looked down at his little purple backpack with the dinosaurs on it, and she thought he might start crying again.

"Mimi never lefted me before. I was scared."

She thought her heart would break. She wracked her brain to think of something to try to make him feel better. "Hey, Andy, how about if we stop and get some ice cream on the way home?"

He shook his head. "I don't want any ice cream. I just wanna go home. I want Mimi."

Chapter Twenty-One

When Victoria unlocked the front door, Andy ran immediately upstairs to his room. He had barely spoken to her the entire ride home. Rather than follow him, she decided to give him some space and let him cool off. It was clear he was upset with her.

Madeline wasn't home yet, so Victoria sat down on the bottom step of the staircase and waited. She glanced at her watch. 2:15. This would be a really long lunchbreak. She just hoped others in the office wouldn't notice how long she'd been gone. Taking long lunches was frowned upon by management, and being a new employee made her doubly nervous about being out half the afternoon.

Her cell phone rang. She dug into her purse and pulled it out. It was Brad again.

"I'm on a break from a meeting," he said. "Did you get him?"

"Yes, I finally found the school and picked him up. We just got home."

"Thank God." She could hear the relief in his voice. "Why were you so late, Victoria? He was crying when I talked to him on the phone."

"I told you, Brad," she almost yelled into the phone. She could feel her temper starting to flare again. "Your mother didn't tell me that school let out early on Wednesdays. I planned on picking him up at 2 o'clock."

Brad paused. "Well, that's not what—"

Victoria broke in. "I don't care what your damn mother says. She didn't tell me."

He paused. "You don't have to take that tone."

"Look, Brad, I'm sorry, but your mother did this on purpose. She's trying to sabotage me with Andy."

Brad sighed. "That's ridiculous, Victoria. Sabotage? So what, now you're believing what Lana tells you?"

"It's the truth, Brad, and if you can't see that—"

He cut her off. "Where is Andy now?"

"He ran up to his room. He's mad at me, just like your mother hoped he would be."

"Well, he needs his afternoon snack, especially since he was so late getting home. He usually has a strawberry and banana smoothie."

She didn't speak as that little fact sunk in. That was the same snack Brad always had when he was hungry. He even had a blender in his hotel room in Las Vegas so he could make them. Victoria couldn't help but wonder if little Bradley also had a strawberry and banana smoothie every day when he came home from school. Was Madeline raising Andy as a Brad clone? Hmmm. Mimi's boys.

"Just like you," she said.

"Yep, just like me."

"Ok, I'll go fix him his snack." She stood up and headed toward the kitchen.

Entering the room, she smelled a delicious aroma coming from the crockpot. She lifted the lid to see beef stew with a lot of vegetables. She guessed that was the dinner Madeline was preparing, dreading the prospect of sharing a meal with two people who didn't care too much for her at the moment.

"Brad, I don't want to eat dinner at the house tonight. I think I'll stay in town and eat out."

197

Brad didn't answer. She thought maybe he'd hung up or they'd gotten disconnected.

"Brad?"

"I don't think that's a good idea?"

She exhaled wearily. "Why not?"

"Because Andy needs consistency in his life, and he needs to learn responsibility. If you don't show up for dinner after what happened today, it will be upsetting to him. He might blame you or feel like you're abandoning him."

She groaned. She knew he was right, but she just wanted to escape having to eat dinner with them tonight. She didn't know if she could handle looking at that smug, self-righteous face of her mother-in-law across the table.

"Promise me you'll be there," Brad said.

She hesitated for a long moment. Then she groaned again. "You know I will," she sighed.

"That's my girl."

She heard the front door slam. "Andrew? Victoria?" her mother-in-law called out.

Victoria said into the phone, "You're mother's here, and I have to get back to work. I'll talk to you later."

"Ok, honey. Chin up. And thanks for picking up Andy."

She hung up and called out, "I'm in here fixing Andy his snack."

Madeline must have broken some kind of speed record getting from the foyer to the kitchen, because when Victoria turned around from the refrigerator, her mother-in-law was hovering right behind her.

"I'll make Andrew his snack," she said, taking the box of strawberries out of Victoria's hands.

Victoria turned around to shut the refrigerator door and rolled her eyes. Madeline just couldn't stand it when she was in her kitchen.

"I have to get back to work anyway," Victoria said. "I've already been gone for over an hour, and I don't want to get in trouble."

Madeline shot her a piercing look. "Well, we wouldn't want that, would we?"

Victoria wasn't in the mood for any of mother-in-law's rebukes. "Well, some of us have to work, Madeline."

"You know, Victoria, there are some things in life more important than work."

Victoria pressed her lips into a line and quickly walked across the room to the kitchen door. "I'm not getting into this with you now, Madeline. I have to get back to work."

She walked out the door and didn't look back.

When she reached the foyer, Andy came running down the staircase and sped right past her toward the kitchen.

"Mimi!" he cried, grabbing his grandmother around the waist and hugging her as she stepped out of the kitchen.

Madeline bent over to hug him, but immediately tilted her head up to peer at Victoria, giving her a smug smile.

Chapter Twenty-Two

Victoria checked the time on her watch as she sat down at her office desk. After 3:00. And, naturally, she'd bumped into her boss in the lobby as she came in the door. Sharon had given her an odd look, but didn't say anything. That just added to Victoria's distress. She was absolutely livid with her mother-in-law for her obvious deceit. And to do it at Andy's expense made it even worse. The poor little thing was so upset.

The rest of her afternoon was shot. She felt so agitated, she couldn't concentrate. She tried to take her mind off it by doing some busy work, tidying some paper files, and organizing her online folders. But mainly she just sat and stared out her window, going over and over in her mind the events of the afternoon and her conversation the night before when Madeline gave her instructions about picking up Andy. She was positive Brad's mother hadn't told her that school let out earlier on Wednesday.

Finally the workday ended, but all she had to look forward to was going home to have dinner with that woman. She found herself poking along the highway, dreading walking through the door. When she passed a big discount store, an idea popped into her head, and she went inside to make a purchase.

When she finally pulled into the driveway, she hoped Andy might be waiting for her on the porch as he usually did. But he wasn't there. Maybe it was because he knew his father was out of town, but somehow Victoria thought it had more to do with him not wanting to see her. That made her feel incredibly sad, much worse than she ever would have thought possible. She really felt like Andy's mother now, with all the emotions that entailed, the emotions she'd never felt before.

She went immediately up to her room, closed the door, and stretched out on the bed. Lying there staring at the ceiling, she wished more than anything that she could "call in sick" to dinner. She looked at the clock—6:20. Moaning as if she were in pain, she forced herself to get up. She flipped through the hangers in the closet and found a light yellow summer sundress that was comfortable and slipped into it.

When she arrived at the table, Andy was already seated, and it sounded like Madeline was in the kitchen. Victoria settled into the chair across from him.

"Hi, Andy."

"Hi," he said, looking down at his lap.

She stared at him for a while, deciding exactly what she was going to say. "You know, Andy, I'm real sorry I was late picking you up from school today. Nobody told me they let you out early on Wednesday."

He didn't look up, but just kept staring down at his lap.

"I thought you got out at 2 o'clock just like you do the other days. I didn't know."

He glanced up at her and then looked down again. "Mimi said she told you and that you don't care about me. That you are iriponsabul."

Victoria could feel the anger starting to rise in her again, but she tried to keep calm as she spoke to her stepson.

"Andy," she said, reaching across the table to take his hand. "I care about you very, very, much. It was just a mistake that you had to wait at the school for so long. Have you ever made a mistake, Andy?"

He continued to stare at his lap, but nodded.

"And after you said you were sorry, did the person forgive you?"

He nodded again.

"Well, Andy, I'm very sorry that I made a mistake and was late getting to school to pick you up. I hope you will forgive me."

He peeked up at her, but didn't say anything.

"Because," she continued, "I love you a lot, and I would never do anything on purpose to hurt you. Do you understand that?"

He nodded slowly.

"Do you forgive me, Andy?"

He blinked his big brown eyes at her several times, and then said softly, "I forgive you."

"Thank you, Andy. Can I get a little smile?"

His lips turned up slightly. It wasn't a complete smile, but it was a start.

Madeline came into the room, holding a big tureen filled with the beef stew that had been cooking in the crockpot earlier that day. Then she left and came back with a basket of garlic bread.

Victoria didn't make eye contact as her mother-in-law ladled stew into each of their bowls and gave instructions to Andy about how to properly eat the stew. Andy reached for a piece of bread and was told to wait until it was passed to him.

Victoria ate silently. The stew was delicious, and normally she would have complimented her mother-in-law on it. But not tonight.

About halfway through the meal, Andy looked at his grandmother and said, "Mimi, I forgived Mommy."

Madeline glanced up from her meal and visibly flinched. She tried to mask her reaction, but Victoria saw it, and Madeline knew she saw it. Victoria couldn't help smiling.

Madeline took her napkin from her lap and dabbed her mouth with it.

"It's forgave, Andrew. Not forgived."

"Oh. I forgave her then."

Victoria smiled and winked at Andrew, waiting to see what else her mother-in-law had to say.

"It's good manners to forgive people when they do something wrong, even when it's very wrong," Madeline said, casting her eyes toward Victoria. "So that was good manners, Andrew."

Victoria rolled her eyes and tried to hold her temper. She felt like leaping across the table at her mother-in-law.

Andy nodded. "I make mistakes too, and I like to be forgave."

"Forgiven," Madeline corrected.

"Forgiven," Andy repeated.

"Andy," Victoria said. "I brought a surprise home for you to let you know how sorry I am."

Andy brightened. "You did? What is it?"

"It's a surprise. I'll show you after dinner."

Andy started rapidly shoveling the stew into his mouth, one spoonful after the other.

Madeline flashed Victoria a dirty look. "Andrew! Slow down and chew your food."

Victoria tried not to laugh. In a few minutes, Andy had finished eating and so had Victoria.

"Ready?" she asked, standing up from the table.

"Ready!"

He took her hand, and they dashed out of the room toward the stairs. Victoria could almost feel Madeline's glare searing a hole in her back.

When they reached the master suite, Victoria opened the bag from the discount store and pulled out a DVD.

"*Finding Nemo*," she said, showing the box to Andy. "Have you ever seen it?"

Andy already was jumping up and down. "I haven't seen it, but I've heard all about it. It seems like everybody else in kindygarden has seen it."

"Well, you're going to get to see it now too!"

Andy sat down on the couch, kicking his legs against the side of it, while Victoria knelt in front of the set, trying to understand how the new built-in DVD player worked. It only took a minute for her to figure it out, and the movie was ready to play.

Before she started it, she told him, "Andy, you have fun watching your movie. I need to have a grown up talk with Mimi. Okay?"

Andy nodded, clapping his hands. "Okay. I'm ready."

Victoria started the movie and sat with Andy for the first few minutes to be sure it was running correctly. Andy quickly became mesmerized and didn't even seem to notice when Victoria said she was leaving the room to go downstairs.

When she reached the kitchen door, she paused to gather herself. This was a conversation with her mother-in-law that she was actually looking forward to having.

Chapter Twenty-Three

Victoria pulled open the kitchen door and stepped in. Her mother-in-law had her back to her, loading the dishwasher. Victoria sat down at the small kitchen table in the corner.

"Madeline, we need to talk."

Madeline turned around and narrowed her eyes at Victoria. "Talk? Talk about what?"

"I think you know what."

Madeline turned her back on her and resumed rinsing some glasses and placing them in the dishwasher.

"Madeline, I've thought back over our conversation last night, and you never told me that I needed to pick up Andy earlier today."

"I most certainly did." She rinsed a plate and placed it in the dishwasher.

"No," Victoria said emphatically, "you did not."

Madeline didn't respond, but continued cleaning the dishes.

"Why do you hate me so much, Madeline, that you'd sabotage me to Brad's son? I don't care what you do to me, but you hurt a little boy. Your own grandson. How could you do that just to get back at me? What did I ever do to you?"

Her mother-in-law glanced over her shoulder. "I didn't sabotage you, Victoria, and I don't hate you."

Victoria snickered. "Oh, c'mon, Madeline. It's just the two of us here. What did I ever do to you? Besides marry your son."

Madeline turned around, dried her hands, and leaned back against the counter. Those intense blue eyes were gleaming.

"You didn't do anything, Victoria. I just don't think you're mother material for my grandson."

Victoria felt her cheeks start to glow and her heart rate speed up. Her Italian temper was about to jump into full gear.

"Oh, is that right?"

"Not only are you irresponsible the one time we ask you to do something for Andrew, but you feed him fattening, sugary foods, let him drink Coke, and let him watch television which will rot his brain. That's what he's doing right now, isn't it?"

Victoria ignored the question. Madeline continued.

"Do you want him to grow up to be unhealthy and overweight like—" she didn't finish her sentence, but she gestured toward Victoria. Victoria sucked in her breath.

"I am not overweight, Madeline!" Victoria screamed, cutting her off. She lowered her voice and tried to control herself. "And just because I don't eat vegetables every meal doesn't mean I have a bad diet. You can eat a little Italian food and have an occasional soft drink without feeling like you're going to balloon into—"

"I'm not surprised you don't understand," Madeline said gesturing at Victoria's figure. "I mean look at you. Those hips, that wild hair, that tacky tattoo for God's sake. What kind of a role model are you? I always hoped Bradley would marry someone more ... refined. More respectable. Who he was proud to show off in public."

Victoria closed her eyes and took a deep breath. She couldn't believe her mother-in-law was saying these things to her.

"Andrew needs a mother with class and style who will raise him in the proper way."

Victoria was livid. Her heart rate was flying and her hands had begun to shake. She took another deep breath and tried to control herself, not sure if she would be able to.

"You know, Madeline, raising a child with rigid rules, denying him the joys that other children experience, will just result in a strange adult who is alienated from other people his age."

Madeline glared at her. "Oh really? Do you think Bradley is strange? Do you think Bradley is alienated? I raised him exactly the same way."

"You know I think Brad is wonderful in every way except for his strange attachment to you. When children grow up, they go out in the world to live their own lives. They don't stay at home with their mothers. Brad is thirty-two years old for God's sake."

Her mother-in-law immediately became defensive. "There is no pressure on Bradley to stay here. He lives here because he wants to."

Victoria laughed out loud. "Give me a break. Bradley feels like he has to stay here. Like he doesn't have a choice, because he doesn't want you to be—"

Suddenly, Victoria felt that she had stepped over the line, that she was being cruel. She stopped mid-sentence and gathered her thoughts.

After a few moments, she said, "Look Madeline, I'm sorry for what you went through when you were growing up. It must have been really, really rough. But everyone has to go through some difficult times in their childhood. Then they get past them and move on. And all mothers have to learn to let go of their children when they grow up—"

Madeline interrupted her. "It *was* hard for me growing up, and that's why I'm so close to my son and my grandson. But I overcame my unfortunate circumstances and look at everything I've accomplished," she said, raising her arms to display the huge room. "But I don't force Bradley to stay here. Bradley's a grown man. He can make his own decisions."

Victoria shook her head. "But he feels guilty. He feels like he's not allowed to leave. And that's not fair to Brad or Andy … or me."

Madeline cocked her head sideways and stared at Victoria. "So, are you saying you want to leave?"

Victoria hesitated but realized the time had come to tell her. "Yes, I want to leave. I'm sorry, Madeline. I know you're Brad's mother and Andy's grandmother, and I want us to visit. Just because we live in another house doesn't mean we can't still be a close family."

She paused, noticing she definitely had Madeline's attention.

"I appreciate everything you've done for us. I truly do. But it's time, Madeline. I can't live under your roof anymore It's not healthy for anyone. We need to get a place of our own."

Madeline dried her hands, and threw the dish towel onto the counter.

"Bradley won't go with you. He's a Reynolds. He loves this house, and he knows his place is here."

"Maybe, maybe not. But I can't continue to live like this. I'm Brad's wife, and he should respect my wishes. And I'm Andy's stepmother. He should be raised by his father and mother. Not his grandmother."

Madeline eyes grew large, and she stared at Victoria for a long moment. Then she rushed out of the room.

Chapter Twenty-Four

The traumatic day and the argument with her mother-in-law left Victoria mentally and emotionally exhausted. All she wanted to do was to get out of that oppressive house and take a walk on the beach to clear her head.

But first, she ran upstairs to check on Andy. As she neared their room, she could hear him laughing.

"How's the movie?" she asked, finding Andy sprawled on his stomach in front of the TV, his chin cupped in his hands.

"It's so funny, Mommy! I love Dory."

He started laughing again, and Victoria waited until he quieted.

"Andy, I'm going to go take a walk on the beach. I'll be back in a little while. Ask Mimi if you need anything."

"Okay," he said, not taking his eyes off the screen. Half-way down the stairs, she heard him break into peals of laughter again.

The second Victoria stepped onto the sand, what she hoped would be a peaceful walk to clear her mind instead became a mass of mental turmoil. How could Madeline call her a bad mother before she'd even had a chance to get used to her new role? She was trying so hard. Sure, she'd made some mistakes, but she already loved that little boy and would never do anything to intentionally hurt him. She knew she had a lot to learn about motherhood, but she would learn. That's what all new mothers had to do, wasn't it? And she'd had a wonderful role model. Her own mother.

The more she thought about their argument and all the hurtful things Madeline had said, the more upset she became. Her mother-in-law thought she was a tacky woman who wasn't good enough to be married to her son or a mother to her grandson. Victoria tried to keep the tears away. She didn't want to let that horrible woman's words get to her that much. But she could feel the tears starting to run her cheeks. Trudging through the sand, staring at her feet, she tried to sweep the tears away, but they just kept coming.

"Whoa there, missy!"

Victoria jolted out of her mental distress and realized she was just a step away from walking over William as he sat in his chair fishing.

"Oh, William, I'm so sorry," she said, swiping the tears away from her face with her arm.

William eyed her blotchy face. "Is everything okay?"

Victoria exhaled wearily and didn't know what to say. "Not really. But I'll get over it."

He stood up and offered her his chair. "I'm a good listener if you want to talk about it. Have a seat."

The offer was tempting. She felt like she really needed to talk to a friend, to unload. But she knew she shouldn't. Not to William. Not to a neighbor.

"I—I shouldn't. It's just family stuff, you know."

He glanced at the Reynolds house. "With that family, there are always problems." He caught her eye. "Serious problems."

"What do you mean?"

"Your mother-in-law."

Victoria sniffled. She wasn't sure if she should say anything or not, but he knew everyone involved and seemed eager to hear what she had to say.

217

"She told me I wasn't mother material. And that she wished Brad had found the right woman, instead of me."

He shook his head. "That sounds like her. Don't you take anything that woman says to heart. She thinks she's the only one who knows how to do anything right."

It felt good to hear someone else say what she was thinking. It seemed that no matter what she did, it was always wrong in Madeline's eyes.

"I can't live like this. I want to move. I want to get our own place, but Brad refuses."

William shook his head. "She's got her claws so deep into him it's pathetic." Seeming to realize he may have offended her, he added, "No harm intended."

She shrugged. "No, I understand," she told him. "I just don't know what to do."

"She's doing the same thing to little Andy that she used to do to Bradley. I hear her bossing him around, bullying him, just like she did with Bradley. They're both scared to death of her."

Victoria furrowed her brow. Madeline must have really done a number on Brad when he was a child for him to still be afraid to cross her when he was thirty-two.

"I just don't understand why she won't let him go. Is she that afraid of being alone? Does she expect Brad to stay with her forever?"

"Selfishness, pure and simple. Wants to control everybody in her life and have everything her own way."

Then a thought occurred to her. "You know, she's European. Maybe that's the way it is in some European families. I know when I visited Italy, there were a lot of multi-generational families living together. Maybe where she's from, the children don't grow up and leave home like they do in America. They stay at home and live with their parents."

William shrugged. "Maybe, but she's been in this country for a long time. And her husband Robert was an American."

"She had such a horrible upbringing, too, losing her parents and having to live in that orphanage where she was mistreated so badly. Brad told me about it. She probably has abandonment issues."

"Hogwash!"

Victoria jerked her head in surprise. "What did you say?"

"I said 'Hogwash!' She wasn't brought up in any orphanage."

"But Brad said—"

"He doesn't know. Bradley's father told me she liked to tell people that so they would feel sorry for her. Robert and I got to be pretty close. He told me her family was upper class over there in Austria and that she was very rebellious against her parents. Unmanageable. A compulsive liar. Promiscuous. Always getting into trouble. When she was sixteen, they sent her to a place to try to straighten her out. I don't think it did any good, but after she got out, she refused to go back home. Said she hated her parents and wouldn't go back. She went to Vienna, where she met Brad's father. She saw him as her ticket out."

Victoria stared at him in disbelief. "What? Are you sure?"

"Positive. It really got on her husband's nerves when she would lie about it."

Victoria was shocked that Madeline had been lying to Brad his entire life about her background, making him feel sorry for her. How could she do that? Victoria couldn't help wondering what Brad would think if he knew.

She glanced back at the house and her heart skipped a beat. Her mother-in-law was standing in the upstairs window, watching them.

"I'd better go, William," she said nervously. "I don't want her to think I'm out here telling you about our argument."

She turned away and started walking through the sand back toward the house.

"You need to get out of there," William called after her.

She stopped and turned back to him. "But Brad won't go."

"Go by yourself then. I'm telling you, you need to get out."

Chapter Twenty-Five

When Victoria reached the master suite, the television set was turned off, and Andy was gone.

She checked her watch. The movie shouldn't be finished yet. She walked down the hallway to the north end of the house to Andy's bedroom door. Brad's mother was in his room, helping him out of his play clothes and into his pajamas.

Victoria spoke to her stepson, ignoring her mother-in-law. "Did you like the movie, Andy?"

Andy looked up at her, a pitiful expression in his eyes. "I really, really liked it, Mommy. But I didn't get to see the end."

Victoria shifted her gaze to her mother-in-law. "It's still early, Madeline. Why wouldn't you let him finish watching the movie?"

"He's watched enough television," she responded, not looking up. "Raise your arms, Andrew."

Andrew silently complied.

"There's no reason he shouldn't be able to finish watching the movie. It's a children's movie, for heaven's sake," Victoria told her.

"I really, really, really liked it." His eyes welled with tears.

"Now is not the time to discuss it, in front of the child," Madeline said sternly. "Andrew, get your storybook. It's time for your bedtime story."

"But it's too early, Mimi. The sun's still out."

"You heard me, Andrew. Do what Mimi says."

Andy looked past her toward Victoria, obviously hoping she would intervene. But Victoria knew if she said anything more, it would turn into a full out war.

"You can watch the rest tomorrow," Victoria told him, blowing him a kiss. She backed out of his room and pulled the door shut behind her. Brad would definitely hear about this tomorrow.

Just who was Andy's mother going to be from here on out? Madeline or Victoria? Victoria was Brad's wife now, and that was her role, a role she expected and wanted. Obviously, Andy's grandmother didn't understand that. She needed to let go and move into the grandmother role and let Brad's wife become Andy's mother. Brad would need to make that clear to her.

Returning to her suite, Victoria looked around for something to do—anything to do—to take her mind off Brad's mother and all the problems that had developed. Spotting her camera, she remembered that it was only a few days until Father's Day, and she wanted to enlarge one of the pictures she'd taken on the beach of Andy flying the kite.

She removed the small disk from her camera and plugged it into her laptop. Pulling up the photos she'd taken that day, she started clicking through them. There were so many good ones that she couldn't decide which one would be best. But she kept being drawn back to the same photo of Andy sitting on Brad's shoulders, flying the kite. Yes, that was the one, she decided.

She was still clicking through the photos when her cell phone rang. It was Brad.

"What in the world is going on there, Victoria?" His voice sounded harsh, more heavy-handed than she'd ever heard it.

"What do you mean, Brad?" she asked, immediately on edge.

"Mother called. She said you confronted her and accused her of purposely hurting Andy by not telling you the right time to pick him up. You know that's not true, Victoria."

What a surprise, Victoria thought. When it comes right down to it, Brad always sides with mommy.

"I suppose you're not interested in my side of the story."

"Of course, I am, Victoria. But can't the two of you get along for just one day when I'm not there?"

Victoria closed her eyes and breathed. She didn't want to argue with her husband and was trying her best to hold her temper. "Brad, your mother sabotaged me by not telling me the right time, and then she told me tonight that I wasn't mother material and she wished you had married somebody else."

There was silence on the phone for several seconds. "Did she really say that?"

Victoria's could feel the heat rushing to her face again. She felt like screaming. But in as calm a voice as she could manage, she asked him, "Do you think I'm lying?"

He immediately responded, "No, no, of course not, honey. I know you're not lying. I, I'm …. sorry my mother said those things to you. I'm sure she didn't mean them. It's just sometimes when she gets angry—"

"Brad, I can't take this anymore. I want to move out."

"No, no, don't say that, honey. We'll work it out when I get home. You'll see."

"I'm not going to change my mind, Brad. I'm done living in this house."

He didn't say anything for a long while, but Victoria could hear that his breathing had gotten heavier. He was almost panting.

"Look, I'll be home Friday. We'll talk about it then."

"We can talk, Brad. But I'm not changing my mind."

He sighed. She could tell he was upset.

"Oh, and Brad, I'm not having another dinner at the table with your mother. I'm also done talking to her, so you can tell her to count me out. I'll eat in town tomorrow night."

"But I wasn't planning on calling her back—" he began.

"Brad!"

He hesitated. "Okay, I'll tell her."

Victoria hung up. She just wanted to take a shower and wash her hair and forget all this drama. But she wasn't quite finished looking through all the photographs, so she wanted to do that first.

Yes, the one with Andy sitting on Brad's shoulders flying the kite was definitely the best one. She would take it in to get it enlarged tomorrow, and buy a frame to fit. It would be the perfect Father's Day gift.

Just about to close her laptop, she noticed the photo she'd taken from the beach of her mother-in-law standing at the window inside the house watching them as they flew the kite on the beach. She remembered the pang of guilt she had felt when she took the picture, when she realized how selfish they'd been not to invite Madeline along with them to the beach, and how alone she looked standing by the window while they were having fun on the beach.

She hit the zoom button to enlarge her mother-in-law's face, hoping that she didn't look too sad standing there alone at the window. Victoria wasn't in the mood to feel sorry for Brad's mother right now.

But when Madeline's face filled the screen, her expression wasn't one of loneliness or sadness. The photograph made Victoria recoil. Her mother-in-law's expression was one of hate, pure unadulterated hate. The picture had captured her real emotions when she thought no one was watching. The look on her face was terrifying. Victoria slammed down the lid of her laptop. She couldn't stand to look at that expression for another second, knowing all that hatred was directed at her.

Chapter Twenty-Six

Victoria awoke the next morning feeling horrible. She hadn't gotten more than an hour's sleep, she was sure of it. Every time she closed her eyes, all she saw was her mother-in-law's hateful stare in that picture. The look in her eyes was beyond hate. It was almost—evil.

Dragging herself out of bed, Victoria opened one eye halfway and glanced in the vanity mirror. Oh God. She looked even worse than she felt—bloodshot eyes, pale, blotchy skin. She couldn't remember the last time she'd had such dark circles under her eyes. And to top it off, she was having a bad hair day. The emotional events of yesterday had taken their toll. She'd give anything if she didn't have to go to work today.

She pulled her hair back into a ponytail with a scarf and piled on concealer and eye makeup. Inspecting her image in the mirror, she saw a tiny improvement, but she still looked awful. Unpresentable really. She considered calling in sick, but after missing half the afternoon the day before, and her boss finding out about it, she couldn't do that.

Anyway, she needed to remove herself from the oppressive atmosphere of this house. She went to the closet and rifled through the hangers. Perhaps reflecting her dark mood, she chose a black dress that she didn't even like, dressed quickly, and hurried out the door without stopping for breakfast. She didn't want to chance running into Madeline.

About halfway to work, she stopped to buy a bagel and a cup of coffee at a coffee shop where she and Brad stopped from time to time, and was just getting settled in at her desk when Kate popped in for their morning chat. She seemed to take a double take at Victoria's appearance.

"Are you not feeling well?" Kate asked, frowning as she squinted her eyes at her.

Victoria rolled her eyes and asked Kate to pull her door shut so they could talk in private.

"You won't believe what's been happening at the house. It's been awful. I don't know what to do."

Victoria related the incident about not being told the correct time to pick up Andy at school.

Kate squinted her eyes shrewdly. "You know what? I'll bet she didn't even have a dentist appointment."

Victoria hadn't even considered that, but at this point, it wouldn't surprise her.

She told her friend about the argument she and her mother-in-law had and what Brad's mother had said about her "not being mother material," and "not the right wife for her son."

Kate gasped. "Are you kidding me? If my mother-in-law said those things to me, I'd go ballistic." She added, "Not that she ever would. She's a real sweetie."

Then Victoria told Kate about the picture she'd taken from the beach when her mother-in-law wasn't aware she was being photographed and the hate-filled expression on her face.

Kate grimaced. "It's obvious she can't stand you. But don't take it personally, Victoria. It sounds like she'd dislike any woman that Brad brought home."

"I think you're right, but when she was saying those horrible things to me, it didn't feel that way."

"You have to get out of there, Victoria. You can't live that way."

Victoria threw her hands up in exasperation. "I know. But what am I supposed to do? I want to move, but Brad refuses. He absolutely refuses to move out of his mother's house."

Kate shook her head. "That's so bizarre, because Brad seems so normal. He's the most popular guy in the office. It's hard for me to imagine him being like that."

Suddenly alarmed, Victoria reminded her friend, "Don't say anything about this around the office, Kate. I don't want people talking about him or thinking any less of him."

Kate cocked her head. "You know I wouldn't that, Victoria. I won't tell a soul."

"I know you won't, I just had to—you know."

"I know," Kate said. "Well, what are you going to do?"

"I don't know. I just don't know. I love Brad so much, but I can't live like this anymore."

Kate thought for a minute. "What if you give Brad an ultimatum? It's either you or his mother?"

Victoria took a deep breath. "I hate to think about which one of us he'd choose. I'm afraid I might come in second in that contest."

"Oh Victoria, don't be silly. I find that difficult to believe. When it comes right down to it, Brad would choose you."

Victoria shrugged. "I'd like to think so, but I'm not so sure about that." She groaned and buried her head in her hands. "Why does this have to be happening?"

Kate reached for the doorknob. "I'd better get back, but let me know if I can help. I'm always here if you need a shoulder to cry on."

Victoria took her hands away from her face and peered up sadly at her friend. "Thanks, Kate. I know I can count on you."

Kate started to leave, but turned back. "Uh, don't take this the wrong way, Victoria, but you look terrible. Why don't you go to the restroom and work on your make-up."

Victoria laughed, despite herself. "Gee thanks."

"Hey, what are friends for?"

After Kate left, Victoria searched her purse for her make-up bag and waited until the coast was clear outside her office to duck into the bathroom down the hall. She didn't want any of her co-workers seeing her looking like this and asking her if she was sick.

Standing at the sink, splashing water on her face, she heard the restroom door open. "Oh, great," she said to herself. "Company."

She didn't look up, but heard a familiar voice. "Looks like somebody had a bad night."

Victoria glanced quickly at Lana, and then back at the mirror. She didn't respond.

"I saw you trying to sneak in here," Lana said, angling her neck sideways to get a better look at Victoria's face. "Wow, you really did have a bad night. Let me guess. Brad's out of town, so it was just you and the dragon lady at home."

How does she even know we're living with Brad's mother? Victoria wondered. "Lana, seriously, I'm not in the mood for this."

"Not easy competing with your mother-in-law for your husband's attention, is it?"

Victoria closed her eyes and tried to block her out. This was the last thing she needed right now.

"What'd she do?"

Victoria shook her head. "Please, Lana. Just leave me alone."

"You can tell me."

Victoria didn't respond.

236

"Trust me. If anyone will understand, it's me."

Victoria knew that was probably true, but she wasn't about to take Lana into her confidence.

Lana continued as if it wasn't a one-sided conversation.

"Yes, if dear Mrs. Reynolds was rough on me, I can only imagine how bad it is for Brad's wives. The last one sure wasn't happy."

Victoria's curiosity got the best of her. She glanced up at her co-worker.

"What do you know about it?"

"Everybody knew that what's-her-name—Erica?—was miserable. She used to call him at the office all the time, bothering him, complaining about his mother. He always had his door shut, arguing with her. She wanted to move out, and he wouldn't."

Victoria cringed at Lana's words, but couldn't resist a dig. "So, how do you know that, Lana? Have your ear pressed to the door eavesdropping?"

Surprised, Lana reddened a bit, but then recovered. "The walls are thin," she answered as a half-baked explanation.

"Well, I don't wonder Andy's mother wanted to move out," Victoria said. "They must have lived there for a long time."

Lana shot her a look of surprise. Then her lips curved upward into a superior little smile.

"You mean Brad hasn't told you?" she asked, a triumphant look in her eye.

Victoria was afraid to ask. She didn't like the sound of Lana's question. "Told me what?" Victoria asked finally.

"Erica wasn't Andy's mother. They weren't even married for a year."

"What?" Victoria couldn't believe what she was hearing. Erica wasn't Andy's mother?

Lana shrugged, and seemed pleased. "So, Brad is keeping secrets. Not surprised. Yeah, when Brad first started working here about five years ago, he was a widower with a little baby boy at home. I was dating someone at the time, or I would have been all over that. But then, he started dating that Erica chick. I think he met her online."

Victoria recoiled at Lana's words. No, no, this wasn't possible! This couldn't be true. Brad would have told her. He wouldn't have kept that from her. Pact or no pact.

Suddenly, her legs began to feel rubbery, like they weren't strong enough to hold her up. She grabbed hold of the wall and leaned her forehead against it. She could feel herself breaking into a cold sweat, and her head started spinning. She reached out toward Lana, and then felt her grabbing her under the arms as she slid to the floor.

Her last thought before she passed out was, "Another wife? Another dead wife?"

Chapter Twenty-Seven

The first sight Victoria saw when she came to was Kate's concerned face staring down at her. Her head was lying on someone's lap. She craned her neck back to see whose it was. Was that Lana?

Her hands dropped onto the cold tile floor, and she tried to sit up. But it made her dizzy, so she leaned back against Lana again and closed her eyes. What had happened?

"Maybe she needs more smelling salts," Lana suggested.

"No, I think she's conscious. Thank God you were able to catch her so she didn't hit her head." Kate eyed Lana suspiciously. "How did you happen to be so close when she fell?"

Lana shrugged innocently. "We were just chatting, you know, girl talk, when all of a sudden her eyes rolled back in her head, and she started to go down."

The door to the restroom opened, and Victoria's boss Sharon walked in. "What in the world happened?"

Victoria tried to speak but the words wouldn't come out.

"She fainted," Lana replied.

"Should we call a doctor?" her boss asked.

"No," Victoria answered, hoarsely.

"Maybe she's pregnant," Lana suggested.

"No, that's not it," Victoria said, looking at her crossly. "I'm just —just not feeling well. I didn't sleep at all last night."

Her boss seemed unsure of what to do.

"Well, if you're sure you don't need to go to the doctor, let's get you home then," Sharon said. "She shouldn't drive, though. Can someone drive her?"

"I can," Lana volunteered. "I know exactly where she lives."

Victoria locked eyes with Kate, sending her a plea for help.

To Victoria's relief, Kate said immediately, "No, I'll drive her. I know how busy you are, Lana."

"I have time. I don't mind," Lana said.

"No, really, Lana. It's okay. I'll take her."

Lana shrugged, obviously disappointed.

Kate patted Victoria's leg. "Let me know when you feel strong enough to get to the car."

Victoria tried to sit up. "Just give me a few minutes."

Fifteen minutes later, they were in Kate's minivan pulling out of the parking lot. To Victoria's embarrassment, half the office watched as Kate and Lana helped her down the hallway to the parking lot.

The first words out of Kate's mouth when they were alone were, "What in the world happened?"

Victoria leaned her head against the passenger side window and muttered, "Lana."

"I knew it! What did she say?"

Victoria sighed. She didn't think she could talk about it right now.

When she didn't answer, Kate said, "Never mind. Just close your eyes and rest."

A half hour later, Kate pulled into the Reynolds' driveway and helped Victoria out of the car and to the front door. When Victoria had trouble getting her key into the lock, Kate took her key chain and opened the door for her.

"Thanks for driving me home, Kate. You're a good friend," Victoria said, starting to close the door behind her.

"Oh no you don't," Kate said. "I'm helping you upstairs."

"It's okay. I can—"

"No. I'm not leaving until I get you tucked safely in bed."

Victoria didn't have the energy to argue. As they crossed the foyer to the staircase, Brad's mother came around the corner from the living room.

Kate took charge. "Oh, hello, Mrs. Reynolds. I'm Kate from the office. Hate to barge in like this, but Victoria got sick at work, and I needed to drive her home."

Victoria didn't say anything or acknowledge her mother-in-law. She just kept walking toward the stairs.

"Oh my. Nothing serious I hope?" Madeline said to Kate. Victoria was surprised. She sounded like she actually cared. Probably a show for Kate, she decided.

"I don't think it's serious," Kate said, "but she needs to get to bed. I'll help her up to her room. The sooner she gets some sleep, the better."

"Of course," Madeline said, graciously extending her arm toward the stairway. "Would some tea help? Or perhaps some soup?"

"Tea might be nice," Kate said. Victoria frowned at Kate the second the words were out of her mouth. She didn't want anything from her mother-in-law.

"On second thought," Kate told Madeline, "tea might keep her awake. She just needs to get some sleep. Thank you anyway."

Madeline shrugged and walked away. Kate put her arm around Victoria to help her up the stairs. Once in the bedroom, Victoria went to her bureau and took out a cotton nightgown. While Kate waited, she went into the bathroom, undressed, and slipped into it. She felt less dizzy now, but tired, so tired. Kate was standing next to the bathroom door when she came out and helped her into bed.

"I'll leave you now so you can get some sleep," Kate said.

Victoria reached out and touched her arm. "Wait, Kate. First, there's something I want you to do for me."

"Sure. Anything."

"Close the door first."

Kate flashed her an interested look, and then walked out into the sitting room to close the door. She also shut the bedroom door behind her. "Okay, what do you need for me to do?"

Victoria felt so weak, but her mind wouldn't rest until she knew more.

She sat up in bed and pointed toward the large walk-in closet. "Way back in the closet over there, on the top shelf in the right-hand corner, there are a couple of photo albums. Would you get them down and bring them to me?"

"Photo albums? You want to look at pictures right now?"

"Please just get them, Kate. I'll explain."

Kate disappeared into the closet and came back carrying two large albums, one in brown leather, the other with a blue vinyl finish.

"What are these?" she asked, setting them on the bed next to Victoria. She fluffed a pillow and climbed onto the bed next to her.

"I'm not sure. I asked Brad about them one time, and he was pretty elusive. I could tell he didn't want to show them to me."

Kate's interest was obviously peaked. "Okay. What are we looking for?"

"I need to verify that something Lana told me is true. I need to see for myself."

Kate pursed her lips. "What did Lana say? This ought to be good."

"She told me that Erica was not Andy's mother. That there was another wife before her."

Kate's mouth dropped open. "Seriously? That's news to me. But then, I don't know Brad all that well, and I only saw Erica at company functions, like the picnic and the holiday party. I just figured she was the little boy's mother."

"That's because you've only been working there for three years. Lana's been there a lot longer. She was there when Brad was hired. She said when he started working there, he was a widower with a baby boy."

Kate gasped. "A widower? You mean he had another wife who—"

Victoria nodded gravely. "Died."

"Oh my God, Victoria."

"Now you understand why I have to see for myself." She picked up the blue album and opened it.

The smiling faces of Brad with his arm around a striking, slender woman with a model-like figure and long, fiery red hair hit Victoria like a punch in the stomach. They were standing on the patio in their bathing suits, the woman dressed in a tiny bikini, vamping for the camera. Suddenly Victoria couldn't breathe and felt as if her face were on fire. She could feel the bile rising in her throat. Maybe she wasn't ready to look at these now.

Kate immediately picked up on Victoria's reaction. She reached over and closed the album cover.

"You shouldn't do this now, while you're not feeling well. It's just going to make you feel worse."

But Victoria couldn't help herself. She opened the cover again. "I have to. I can't think about anything else."

She looked again at the wife with the long red hair and the super model body. Was this Erica? Or was it Andy's mother? When she turned the page, that question was answered. There was Andy, about a three-year-old version, sitting on her lap. This woman had to be Erica, the bicycle rider.

She closed the album. She couldn't stand to look at any more.

"That was Erica."

"Yes," Kate agreed. "I remember her."

Setting the blue album aside, she picked up the brown one and sat staring at it. "Another wife, another album?"

Kate exhaled. "Victoria, don't put yourself through this."

Instead of replying, Victoria opened the cover and found herself staring down at the most delicate, angelic looking bride she'd ever seen. Dressed in a gorgeous lace wedding gown with a long train, the woman wore a wreath of flowers that looked like a halo in her long, silky blonde hair. A much younger Brad stared at her adoringly, as if he'd never seen such a beautiful sight. They each had several attendants. It looked like it was a huge wedding.

This time, Victoria did get sick. She jumped out of bed and ran to the bathroom. After she'd finished heaving what little she had in her stomach, she stared at herself in the mirror and realized she was shaking. Uncontrollably.

Kate rapped on the bathroom door. "Victoria? Are you all right?"

"I'm...all right. I'll be out in a minute." She washed her face, scrubbed her hands, and studied herself in the mirror. Her cheeks were drawn, her eyes deep set and dark, her mouth downturned. It made her feel even worse to look at her reflection. All she could think of, was that she looked like death.

She opened the bathroom door, and Kate helped her back to the bed.

"Okay, that's it," Kate said. "No more photo albums. You need to get some sleep."

"I will. I just need to look for one more thing. Then, I'll stop."

She pulled the brown album onto her lap again and flipped forward a couple of pages. There she found a photo of the blonde woman, very pregnant and holding her stomach, smiling shyly for the camera. She looked lovelier than ever. And then, the oh-so-proud parents holding the baby, only a couple of months old, but so obviously little Andy.

So, this gorgeous woman—Victoria didn't even know her name—was Andy's mother. Looking closer, she could see the resemblance, especially in the eyes. How blessed Andy was to have the genes of those two perfect human specimens. But what had happened to this woman, Andy's angelic-looking mother? She was so young and vibrant. How in the world did she die?

Chapter Twenty-Eight

Kate left soon afterward, setting the photo albums on the end table as Victoria asked her to so she could look at them again later. As upset as Victoria was about what she had discovered, she drifted off to sleep quickly, exhaustion overtaking her.

She wasn't sure how long she'd been asleep, when something awakened her. Suddenly alert, she noticed movement by the window. Someone was in the room with her. The drapes were drawn, so she squinted through the semi-darkness. An immobile figure stood in the shadows a few feet from the bed, staring down at her. Victoria bolted upright when she realized it was her mother-in-law.

"What are you doing in here?" she demanded, clutching the sheets to her chest, wondering how long Brad's mother had been standing there watching her.

Madeline stepped forward. "I was just checking on you."

The woman's manner made her feel uneasy. "I'm…I'm fine. I just need to sleep."

"I thought you might like some soup." Madeline nodded toward the small table by the window where a large soup bowl sat on a serving tray.

Victoria glanced at it. "Well, thank you, but what I need now is to sleep."

"No, let me get it for you. You need to keep up your strength." She picked up the tray and stepped toward Victoria. She bent over to put in on Victoria's lap.

Victoria held up her hand to her mother-in-law. "Thank you, Madeline, but I'm not hungry. I just want to sleep."

Madeline seemed disappointed. "Suit yourself. But I'll leave it here in case you change your mind. You need to keep your strength up."

She stood for a second more, staring oddly down at Victoria, and then started to move toward the door. But she stopped when she noticed the photo albums on the end table.

A small smile crept onto her face. "I see you were looking at pictures of Bradley and Marie."

Victoria glanced self-consciously at the albums and wished she had followed Kate's suggestion to put them back up in the closet. She didn't answer.

"What a sweet girl Marie was," her mother-in-law continued. "Such a perfect wife for Bradley. They made the most beautiful couple."

Victoria wouldn't give her mother-in-law the satisfaction of knowing how much her words hurt her, how much they pierced her to the core. Instead, she rolled over on her side, turned her back on Brad's mother, waited for her to leave the room.

But her mother-in-law wasn't quite finished. She had one more parting shot. "Yes, Marie was the love of Brad's life."

When Victoria heard the door click shut, she couldn't hold back the tears. Clutching a pillow to her chest, curling into the fetal position, she sobbed so hard that her shoulders heaved. She cried until she felt as if she didn't have an ounce of energy left in her body. Then, miraculously, she fell asleep again.

She slept for hours, stirring only when a warm little hand touched her arm.

"Mommy," Andy whispered.

Her eyes slowly opened to see Andy's little face, filled with concern.

"Hi, Andy."

"I'm sorry you're sick, Mommy."

She rolled on her side to face him, holding up her head with her palm. "Thank you, Andy. That's so sweet of you."

"What's the matter?" He put his hand on her forehead.

"Oh, it's nothing serious. I'll feel better tomorrow."

"Do you have a tummy ache?"

"I did. But not anymore. It went away."

He glanced over at the table.

"You didn't eat your soup. Mimi says it's good to eat soup when you're sick."

"That's true. But I just wasn't hungry." Victoria yawned and stretched her arms. "Thank you for coming to visit me, Andy."

"You're welcome. I'm going to go play now."

"Ok. Have fun."

Victoria rolled over and tried to fall asleep again, but sleep wouldn't come. Her mind kept replaying the pictures she'd seen in the photo albums, bouncing back and forth between the vivacious redhead and the sweet little blonde bride. The love of his life. The most beautiful couple. Those pictures made her feel so ordinary, so unimportant, so—nothing. She was just wife number three, nothing special, just a tacky, less attractive substitute for the wife that he really deserved.

She could feel herself slipping, and she knew she was on the brink of another bout of tears. Throwing back the bedspread, she forced herself to get out of bed and take a shower. Maybe feeling clean would make her feel human again.

The hot spray from the five shower heads slowly pushed away most of the disturbing thoughts that were tormenting her, relaxing both her body and her mind. She washed her hair, shaved her legs, and took her time covering her damp body with a soothing lotion to soften her skin.

Slipping into her terry cloth robe, she wiped steam off the mirror and took a visual inventory. Much improved. The dark circles under her eyes were almost gone and the steamy shower had given her face a healthier glow. She spent a few minutes putting on some makeup and combing and drying her hair.

When she finally stepped out of the bathroom, she looked across the room and screamed. Brad was sitting on the edge of bed, the brown photo album balanced in his lap.

"Brad, what are you doing here? I thought you were in Tampa."

His eyebrows furrowed into a frown, and he looked up at her suspiciously.

"I thought you were sick? You don't look sick to me."

Still stunned that he was back and had caught her with his photo albums, her words stumbled out. "I—I was sick. I fainted at work. But I'm feeling better now. Who told you I was sick?"

His voice still cold, he answered. "When I called in to work, Sharon told me."

"Oh," she murmured.

"I came rushing back." He sounded more irritated than concerned. "What happened? Where were you when you fainted?"

"I was in the restroom talking to Lana."

Brad rolled his eyes and shook his head. "That bitch! What did she say to you?"

Victoria let her eyes drop to the album. Brad reddened. He set the album aside and walked over to her, taking her by the arms.

"I didn't want you to find out like that. I was planning to tell you."

"What? That you have two dead wives, not just one?"

He let go of her and gave her a sharp look. "Thanks for the sympathy." His voice was laced with sarcasm. "It hasn't been easy."

Victoria immediately regretted her surly comment. "I'm sorry. I didn't mean to be unkind."

"It's not something that's easy for me to talk about."

"You mean Marie?"

He glanced at her, surprised that she knew his first wife's name. Victoria couldn't stop from adding, "The love of your life."

Brad immediately stepped forward and took hold of her arms. "Don't say that, Victoria. It's not true. You're—"

She cut him off. "Don't Brad. Your mother has already told me what a wonderful couple you were, and I can see by looking at the pictures how in love with her you were."

"My mother doesn't know anything about it. Anyway, it was a different kind of love. You know, first love. You and I have so much more in common. We have a much more mature love. "

Victoria wasn't sure if she liked the sound of that, but she didn't argue the point. There was something more important that she wanted to know. "What happened to her, Brad?"

He started pacing the room. "It's not easy for me to talk about. That's why I haven't told you before."

Victoria stood silently, waiting for a response. He finally stopped pacing, sat down on the bed, and put his head in his hands.

"She committed suicide."

Victoria inhaled a deep breath. "Suicide?"

He looked up at her and nodded. "Post-partem depression. Andy was only four months old."

Victoria sat down at the dressing table. "My God. How awful for you."

"The worst experience of my life."

"How did she—"

Brad squeezed his eyes shut as if he were trying not to visualize the scene. He didn't respond for several seconds. Finally, he pointed to the hallway. "She jumped over the railing."

Victoria's hands flew to her mouth, and her eyes traced the line from where she was sitting across the suite to the second floor railing, not thirty feet away. "Oh my God! How terrible."

"It was horrible."

"Did you see her do it?"

He shook his head, and tears welled in his eyes. "No, I was in bed asleep."

Victoria could see that telling the story was upsetting him, but she also knew that this might be her only chance to get some answers that she wanted to know.

"Were there signs, you know, ahead of time?"

He nodded, his faced sagging. "There were, but I didn't really pick up on them. Not enough."

"Had she been to the doctor about it?"

Brad nodded. "She was on medication. She had just been to the doctor a week before."

"Was there an inquest? Did the police come?"

He shot her a surprised look. "Of course, the police came." There was an irritated edge to his voice. "They did a full investigation. It was ruled a suicide."

Something about the way he answered sent a chill down her spine. He must have noticed her reaction, because he asked her, "You believe me, don't you?"

She wasn't sure if she did or not and was slow to answer. "Is there a reason I shouldn't?"

Chapter Twenty-Nine

It was obvious that Brad thought he'd said enough and didn't want to talk about it anymore. He immediately left the bedroom to go downstairs. Victoria didn't go with him. She went back to bed to rest, and think. Still reeling from the sad news about Andy's mother, she wasn't sure what to believe anymore.

Brad's secrecy and odd behavior made her feel edgy and unsure if she even wanted to stay with him. He had been married to two women before, both of whom he was obviously crazy about based on the photos she'd seen, and they both had died mysteriously. Did Marie really commit suicide? Who ran Erica down? Were they just unrelated incidents, or was there something sinister going on?

She found it difficult, if not impossible, to believe that her sweet Brad could be involved in anything nefarious. But it was all so suspicious. She had begun to feel uncomfortable even being in this house, in this bed. Was she in danger? Maybe she should visit the police department to see what they had to say about the deaths of Brad's first two wives.

She lay awake for two hours running over and over in her mind everything she now knew, trying to convince herself that her husband couldn't possibly have anything to do with the deaths of his previous wives. He couldn't, she decided finally. Not her Brad.

She thought he would have returned to the room by now, but he was still downstairs. Undoubtedly, he was getting an earful from his mother about what a terrible wife she was. But honestly, she just didn't care anymore now that she knew who Brad's mother really was, and what her motivations were. She had even lied to Brad about her upbringing, not that Victoria would ever tell him. How could you lie to your own son about something like that?

But Victoria was determined she wouldn't have to put up with the lies and the sabotage much longer. She was moving out of this house, this mausoleum, and getting a place of her own. She hoped that she'd be able to convince Brad to come with her once he understood how Madeline was treating her. But even if he didn't, she was moving out. She would tell him tomorrow when they were away from the house.

She fell asleep early, before Brad returned to the room, and despite sleeping most of the day, she slept soundly through the night. When she awoke early the next morning, she felt refreshed, rested, and eager to get back to work and out of that house.

She and Brad barely spoke as they dressed for work. But when they sat down at the kitchen table to drink a cup of coffee, Brad opened a manila envelope he had carried into the room with him, and pulled out a document.

"Here's the life insurance policy we talked about. It covers each of us for two million dollars." He pointed to the bottom line and took a pen out of his pocket. "You sign here. I'll fax it to them when we get to work, and it will go into effect today."

Victoria could feel her pulse rate shoot up. She stared at the document, and then at Brad. Did she really want to sign this? Her husband had been married twice before, and now both of his wives were dead. Did he have insurance policies on them too?

"Is something wrong?" Brad asked, eyeing her as he extended the pen.

Her throat had gone dry, and she felt short of breath. "I'm not sure I want to do this, Brad."

He frowned. "I thought we had discussed this and were in agreement?"

When her eyes rose to meet his, he could see the fear on her face.

"What?" He looked at her as if he didn't understand. Then the realization hit him. "Are you kidding me? Is that what you think of me? That I'm going to kill you for the insurance money?"

She blinked and swallowed, not sure what to say. As he stared down at her, his expression changed from one of anger to hurt and disappointment. He started to pick up the policy. "If that's what you really think of me, then forget it. Just forget it. This is more to protect you than me."

As he started to step away, she reached out and quickly took the pen from his hand. "No, no, of course not," she said. "Where do I sign?"

She had decided the night before that she was going to trust her husband and this was part of it. She was sure she had nothing to worry about.

On the drive to work, they barely spoke. She knew he was still upset about her hesitance to sign the insurance papers. But as they neared the office, Victoria knew she needed to talk to him about another subject—moving.

"Brad, I want to move, and I want to move now. Your mother hates me, she's begun to sabotage me, and she's trying to turn Andy against me. I can't stand living under her roof anymore."

Brad didn't react. He kept his eyes straight forward on the road. "I think you're exaggerating, Victoria. Mother wouldn't do that. We talked about it last night. She said she still didn't see how you could have misunderstood."

"Misunderstood? She purposely sabotaged me, Brad. And I can't tell you how much it bothers me that you're taking her side."

He sighed as if he were lecturing an unruly child. "Victoria, my mother didn't sabotage you. The two of you are just going through an adjustment period. She's been used to being in the mother role with Andy, and then suddenly you show up. I'm sure that's upsetting to her, and she might be a little jealous."

"This goes way beyond an adjustment period, Brad. And she's more than a little jealous. I told you the horrible things she said to me. And now she's so hell bent on making me look bad that she's even doing things that hurt Andy. That whole school fiasco was a total setup."

"Seriously, Victoria? Maybe you do watch too much TV."

Victoria crossed her arms in front of her and tried to keep her temper from flaring. She turned to stare out the window. "You are so blind where your mother is concerned."

Brad shook his head. "I just know her. She would never do something like that."

Victoria sighed with disappointment. How naïve could her husband be?

They didn't speak for the rest of the drive until Victoria remembered something that Kate had said. It was a last-ditch effort but worth a try, Victoria decided.

"Brad, what if your mother didn't have an appointment at the dentist? What if her asking me to pick up Andy on a day when she knew the schedule was different was a ruse to make me look bad? Would you believe me then?"

"Look, Victoria, if my mother said she had a dentist appointment, she had a dentist appointment."

"Well, why don't you call the dentist and at least check? Do you know which dentist she goes to?"

Brad's tone was dismissive. "We've gone to the same dentist for years, Dr. Jenkins. But that's not the point, Victoria. My mother wouldn't lie, and I don't feel right about sneaking around behind her back checking up on her."

"Well, I don't see it as sneaking around," Victoria insisted. "You're hearing two different versions of this story. You would just be doing a little background checking. Otherwise, it seems to me that you just take your mother's word for everything. That you're choosing her over me."

"Now that's not fair—"

"Look, Brad. Just call the dentist. If your mother had an appointment, I'll stop saying she tried to sabotage me. But if she didn't have an appointment, then she definitely set me up, and I want to start house hunting today." She didn't say that she would be starting to hunt for a new place anyway, with or without him.

Brad didn't answer for a long while. "I'll think about it," he said, finally.

When they pulled into the parking lot, Lana, of all people, was just arriving for work too. Brad immediately marched over to her.

"You leave my wife alone. Stop upsetting her at work." He was actually pointing his finger in her face. Victoria had never seen him so angry.

A little smile appeared on Lana's lips, and she shrugged with seeming disinterest.

"It's not my fault you're keeping secrets from your wife."

"My marriage is none of your concern."

Lana obviously was enjoying the confrontation. "From the looks of her yesterday, your mother is about to run off another one."

Brad took a step toward her. "Don't you talk about my mother either. Stay out of my business, Lana."

Lana turned her back on him and walked toward the office entrance. Looking back over her shoulder, she said, "I'm just glad I got out when I did. Your family situation is way too weird for me."

Brad had his hands on his hips, pacing around the parking lot, kicking every stone in his path. Victoria had never seen him so furious. She took hold of his arm when he started to follow Lana inside. "Just let it go, Brad.

Don't make it worse. You're not going inside the building until you calm down."

He took a deep breath and started pacing again. She leaned on the car, waiting for his temper to subside.

"Ready to go in?" she asked finally.

"I don't know. I guess so. That woman—"

"Now don't get yourself worked up again. When we go inside, you have to be a professional."

"I know, I know."

As they walked into the building, Victoria couldn't help but wonder what made Brad the angriest, Lana telling her about Marie, or talking about his mother?

She had a lot of work to catch up on after going home sick the day before, so she buried her nose in paperwork and was making real progress when Brad unexpectedly tapped on her door.

"What is it?" Victoria asked.

"I called the dentist," he told her, a sheepish expression on his face. He stepped inside her office and shut the door. "My mother didn't have an appointment."

Thrilled that Brad had even called the dentist, Victoria felt vindicated that he now realized that his mother was lying.

He sat down across from her and shook his head. "I can't believe my mother would do that to you. And to Andy. She denied it and denied it and denied it."

The guilty expression on his face made her heart melt.

"Thank you, Brad. You don't know how much it means to me for you to say that."

"And all those other hurtful things she said to you," he said. "That you weren't a good mother and that she wished I'd married somebody else. That just makes me sick."

Victoria nodded but didn't respond.

"I'm just so sorry. I should have believed you from the beginning. Can you ever forgive me?"

She wanted to rush around the desk and hug him but, since they were at work, she reached across her desk and took his hand. "Of course, I forgive you, Brad."

"Thank you, honey. I don't deserve you."

Victoria let go of his hand lest her boss or a co-worker pass by the glass window that looked out into the office area. "Do you understand why I want to move? Why I can't live under her roof?"

"I do. I mean, I know she's jealous and she's not being herself. Maybe it *was* too much for me just to show up without warning with a new wife. But still—"

"Look, Brad. We'll still have a relationship with your mother after everything calms down. We'll still see her. But we can't live with her. We need to move out. And right away."

When Brad nodded in agreement, Victoria felt a huge rush of relief. She couldn't believe he had finally agreed to move out. She wasn't going to take any chances that he might change his mind.

"I'll go online during lunch and start looking for some places. Maybe we could go house shopping tomorrow."

He started to agree, but then thought of something. "Today is Andy's last day of kindergarten. Then he's off for the summer. Who's going to watch him while we're at work?"

Victoria had already considered that and was ready with an answer. "We're going to have to hire someone to watch him after school anyway. We can start looking right away for the right person. And maybe we can find him a little summer camp around town to go to this summer. If we can find a place close enough to the office, we can come home for lunch and spend time with him then too."

Brad didn't look convinced. "Or maybe my mother could watch him, and I could pick him up after work?"

Victoria shook her head. "No. I don't feel comfortable with that. Your mother will just keep running me down to him. I'm sorry, Brad, but at the moment, I just don't trust her. Maybe sometime down the road I'll feel differently, but not now."

He didn't look convinced.

"We have to make the break sometime, Brad. And that may mean having to get sitters or putting Andy in an afterschool program. But a lot of parents do that, and their kids turn out just fine. It's better than having him bullied by his grandmother and having her undermine his parents to him."

From the unsettled expression on Brad's face, Victoria wasn't sure if she'd gotten through to him or not. He sat staring out her office window, thinking about it for a long while.

"Yes," he said finally, a look of determination on his face. "It's time."

Chapter Thirty

Ecstatic at the prospect of moving out of Madeline's house and buying her own home, Victoria immediately went online and began to search for houses for sale in Jacksonville, not too far from the office. She would have loved to live in St. Augustine, but it was just too long of a commute to work. Knowing Brad and Andy's love for the ocean, she zeroed in on the beach communities of Jacksonville Beach and nearby Neptune Beach.

She felt a little guilty that she basically blew off work all afternoon to search on real estate websites for a new home, especially after going home sick the day before. But she couldn't help it. This was too important to her, and she was too excited to do anything but shop for a house. She even lined up a real estate agent for Saturday to show them several of the houses that caught her eye.

273

They agreed not to say anything to Madeline or Andy until they found a place they liked and were ready to move. Victoria focused on homes that were rent to own, or were available to rent before the house closed, so they could move immediately. She couldn't bear the thought of another month or two in Madeline's house while they waited for their house to close.

But while she was glued to her computer house shopping, an unpleasant thought, a very unpleasant thought, kept sneaking into her brain. She did her best to push it away, but it kept coming back. Now that Brad had finally agreed to move out, she didn't want to think about the mysterious deaths of Marie and Erica—and the fact that he had been less than up front with her about them.

She thought long and hard about it, and finally decided to accept his explanations about what had happened to them and to suspend the suspicion she had initially felt. It was just beyond her comprehension that her sweet, gentle Brad could have had anything to do with their deaths. The very thought was outrageous. He had just been the victim of horrible bad luck. That happened to some people. But she did decide that if anything happened again to make her suspicious, she would go to the police.

After all these weeks of having to live with Brad's mother, and all her cruel, insensitive insults, Victoria was elated that it would soon be over. They would still visit his mother, and she could come to visit them, but they would no longer be living under her roof. Eventually, when Madeline accepted her role as Andy's grandmother, not his mother, they would evolve into a normal relationship and bad feelings would be forgotten. Well, maybe not forgotten, but forgiven. Victoria had never been one to hold grudges, and she certainly wasn't going to start to now. Especially with Brad's mother. In time, everything would calm down. She felt sure of it.

On Saturday morning, Brad and Victoria drove to Jacksonville Beach to meet with their real estate agent, telling Brad's mother that they had several errands to run. She was still avoiding Victoria, and didn't ask her about it, but Victoria could tell that she was suspicious and heard her quizzing Brad about what kind of errands they had that would take the entire day.

The young real estate agent, whose name was Noah, had so many houses to show them that they needed to narrow down the list based on the location, the size of the home, and the selling price. They ended up looking at five different houses that fit their criteria, and found pros and cons with each.

But Victoria fell in love with a recently renovated two-story Cape Cod that was one block from the ocean in Neptune Beach. It had four bedrooms and two baths, a huge living room, modern kitchen, big deck for barbequing, and a fenced-in back yard. The house also had a glassed-in Florida room and a bonus room upstairs that would be perfect as a playroom for Andy. And, best of all, the owners had moved out and were willing to rent it immediately until the sale went through.

Victoria was ecstatic, Brad less so, but still willing. She could see that he was trying to appear enthusiastic as they viewed houses that were far smaller and less elegant than where he had lived his entire life. He had begun to waver again and seemed disappointed that they couldn't find anything in their price range right on the beach other than a small one-bedroom condominium that would never work for the three of them.

The agent encouraged them to make an offer that day, explaining that houses so close to the ocean went quickly. Victoria was excited to put in an offer and didn't want this perfect home to get away from them. But Brad kept coming up with one reason after the next of why they should wait—interest rates might go down, he wanted to look at more houses, they could save for a bigger down payment.

Only when they seemed at a standstill, and Victoria asked the agent to show her some smaller properties that she could afford on her own, did Brad come around. She would never forget the look of shock he had given her, which she countered with a determined, "I'm moving. If you want to stay, stay. But I'm moving."

But even after that, he wanted to put in an offer on the house that was so ridiculously low, that there was no way the owner would accept it.

Victoria knew he wanted them to lose the house. But she stubbornly insisted they offer more and told Brad privately again that she was moving out of his mother's house within the next few days whether he was coming with her or not.

Brad finally relented, and they made an offer on the home in the amount the real estate agent suggested. They would learn tomorrow if their offer was accepted.

Victoria was elated and wanted to go out to dinner to celebrate. Dinner out also had the added benefit of not having to endure another awkward meal around

Madeline's table. Brad called home to tell his mother and Andy that they wouldn't be home until later that evening.

As she sipped on a margarita at a beachfront seafood restaurant that was walking distance to what might become their new home, Victoria could talk of nothing else than whether their offer was high enough and if it would be accepted. She just wished that Brad was as enthusiastic about it as she was. He seemed nervous and distracted, and each time she brought up the house, he tried to change the subject.

He'll come around, Victoria told herself. It's going to be a major change for him, but as soon as we get moved in, he'll see how perfect it is for the three of us. Yes, he'll come around.

Chapter Thirty-One

It was Father's Day, and Victoria may have been even more excited about it than Brad was. She awoke with a feeling of happiness and excitement that she hadn't felt since their wedding today. Part of it was making the offer on the house, she knew, but she hadn't celebrated a Father's Day since she was a child. She wanted Brad to have a perfect day, and she couldn't wait for him to see the framed picture she had taken of him and Andy flying the kite.

After dinner the night before, they stopped in the nice grocery store that Victoria had fallen in love with and bought huge T-bone steaks, corn on the cob, and baked potatoes for their Father's Day cookout. Victoria wanted it to be a nice, relaxing day at the beach, watching Brad surf and playing with Andy. Brad's mother would be there, of course, but Victoria was determined not to let anything the woman did or said get to her. If everything went as she hoped, tonight would be her last one under her mother-in-law's roof. She couldn't wait to hear from the real estate agent to see if their offer had been accepted. Brad had agreed that if it was, they would take a vacation day off work on Monday to move into their new home.

When Brad went downstairs for breakfast, Victoria changed into her pink bathing suit and white cover-up and then pulled out the framed photo of Brad carrying Andy on his shoulders as he flew the kite. Taking out the wrapping paper and card she'd bought a few days earlier during lunch, she started to wrap the gift just as Andy came into the room.

"What is it? What is it?" he asked, clapping his hands.

Victoria thought for a minute whether she wanted to surprise Andy too, but then decided it would be a much better gift if it were from her and Andy. After all, Brad was Andy's father.

She hadn't taped the package yet, so she carefully unwound the striped blue wrapping paper and pulled out the picture.

"What do you think? Do you think Daddy will like it?"

Andy nodded his head proudly. "I remember that. I was flying the kite from way up on Daddy's shoulders."

Victoria rewrapped the package, aided by Andy who applied the tape exactly where she told him too. Then she opened the Father's Day card, signed it, and handed the pen to Andy to sign the card too.

Andy carefully printed each letter of his name and then drew a smiley face next to it.

"Andy, that looks great! You're such a good printer."

Andy beamed. "I know. I've been practicing at kindygarden."

"Do you want to seal the envelope?"

Andy nodded, licked the adhesive on the envelope, and then pressed the back flap shut with his palm. Victoria slipped the card under the ribbon tied around the package.

"Let's take it downstairs and hide it so Daddy won't know we got him a present," Victoria told him. "Shhh. No telling."

"Shhh," Andy said, placing his index finger on his lips.

The weather was gorgeous and the waves huge by North Florida standards. They couldn't have asked for a more beautiful scene for Brad to have his special day. He spent the afternoon surfing while Victoria helped Andy build a sand castle near the shore.

But she had trouble keeping her eyes off Brad. Dressed in aqua blue swim trunks, his tanned muscles rippling as he balanced on the board, her husband was putting on quite a show. Not only did he look great, but he was an amazing surfer. More times than not, he rode the wave all the way into shore and jumped off the board on his own rather than being knocked off.

He gave Andy a short lesson, and actually was able to get his son to ride a wave for several feet. It was obvious to Victoria that someday Andy would be just as talented as his father. Then Brad tried to give Victoria a lesson. That was a laugh. She had little enthusiasm and even less balance. After two disastrous attempts, she gave up and left the surfing to her husband.

When they returned to the patio, the grill was fired up, and Madeline had prepared a couple of side dishes and a salad to accompany the steaks and corn on the cob. Under Madeline's critical eye, Victoria cooked the steaks for her husband on the grill, while Brad and Andy played catch in the pool. Victoria tried to ignore her mother-in-law, but it was difficult under the nonstop stream of instructions about the proper grilling of steaks.

They finally enjoyed a delicious Father's Day barbeque around the stone picnic table under the shade of a huge umbrella. Brad told Andy about some of the Father's Days he remembered with his father when he was a child, spent in a similar manner to what they were doing today. Madeline even chimed in with a few observations. It was obvious how close Brad and his father were, and how much Brad had adored his father.

When they finished eating, Victoria excused herself and retrieved the gift, secretly handing it to Andy. He hid it behind his back and presented it coyly to Brad, and then helped him unwrap it. Brad was thrilled with the photograph, gave Victoria a kiss, and told her how talented she was. Then he suggested to Andy that they go fly the kite again.

Victoria didn't feel as uncomfortable as she thought she would being left alone with Madeline to clean up. Victoria said little, other than to compliment some of the food Madeline had prepared. Now that her time in the house was nearly over, the oppressive atmosphere seemed to lift, and nothing Madeline said really bothered her much anymore.

Brad and Andy had run far down the beach flying the kite, so after everything was cleaned up, Victoria decided to walk down to join them. As she started toward them, she passed William in his usual spot on the beach.

"You're still here?" he asked, obvious concern in voice. "I thought you said you were going to leave."

"We are!" Victoria told him excitedly. "We just made an offer on a house. We're waiting to hear if it was accepted."

"Does she know?" he asked, nodding toward Madeline's house.

"Not yet."

"Listen to me, Victoria. Get out of the house and get out now before she has an inkling that you're moving. I don't trust that woman."

"I am going, William. Just as soon as the house comes through."

"That may not be soon enough. Go now."

"Believe me, William, the sooner the better. I can't wait to get out of that house. But we have to have somewhere to go."

William looked troubled, as if he couldn't decide whether he should say something or not.

"What is it?" she asked.

"I've been going back and forth on whether I should tell you this. There was never any proof, not enough for the cops to make an arrest."

Victoria felt a chill go down her spine.

"What are you talking about?" she asked, dreading to hear his answer.

He turned to stare out at the ocean. Then he looked back and told her seriously, "She's dangerous. Especially when things don't go the way she wants them to."

"What do you mean?" She realized her voice was quivering. She could feel her fear growing by the second.

He hesitated again, as if he were about to tell her something he knew he shouldn't. Then he blurted it out.

"I think she killed her husband. Brad's father."

Victoria stared at him in disbelief. She could feel her skin beginning to prickle and suddenly her body was covered with a cold sweat.

"Why would you think that, William?"

"Because Brad's father told me the day before he died that he was divorcing her. He'd had enough. But he couldn't figure out how to get her out of the house. It was his family home, and he didn't want to lose it."

William paused, recalling the day twenty years before. "She was furious. I could hear her screaming at him from all the way down the beach. Bradley was off at some summer camp, so he wasn't there to see it. Then, the next thing I hear, Robert's dead. He was only forty-two years old. He didn't have any heart attack."

"What do you think happened?"

He gave her a meaningful stare. "I think she poisoned him."

"Poison?" Victoria sucked in her breath. All she could think about was the soup her mother-in-law had brought her. She thought it was strange at the time, the way she stood in the shadows, staring at her while she slept. Madeline had woken her up just to give the soup to her. And she had been so insistent that she eat it.

William continued, "I told the police everything Brad's father told me, and they were suspicious all right. But they never could find any poison."

Victoria looked at him hopefully. "Well, maybe he did have a heart attack."

William shook his. "She killed him. I know she did. They just could never prove it."

Victoria didn't say anything for a few moments, trying to process everything he'd told her. Then she stared questioningly at William.

"But what about you, William? If you think she did that, that she's dangerous, aren't you ever afraid of her? If she thinks you know, do you think she might come after you?"

William shook his head. "Not really," he said quickly. "She's known for years that I suspect her, and she knows I've contacted the police about her more than once. I think she's smart enough to realize that if anything ever happened to me, she would be their first suspect."

He stopped talking and focused his stare on her again.

"But you need to get out of there. Two other young women have already died under suspicious circumstances. I'm not saying she's responsible, but who knows what happened to them? If you know what's good for you, missy, you'll get out of there as fast as your legs will take you."

As she started to walk away, he called after her, "When things don't go her way, look out."

Chapter Thirty-Two

Victoria didn't know what to think. She knew her mother-in-law wasn't a nice person and that she had some weird attachment issues. But a murderer? That was hard to believe. Was William's imagination getting the best of him? Or was Brad's mother truly dangerous? She glanced back at the house, and saw her mother-in-law standing on the patio, watching her again, watching them talking. It felt strange and uncomfortable.

Brad and Andy were approaching in the distance, so Victoria walked toward them. She wanted to tell Brad what William had told her, but it didn't feel right somehow. How could she accuse Brad's mother of murdering his father without proof? And on Father's Day of all days. He wouldn't believe her. He'd defend his mother. And then Victoria would be vulnerable. If her mother-in-law was a murderer, she would know Victoria suspected her.

No, she decided. She would keep her mouth shut, but remain alert. More than alert. Vigilant. And she wouldn't eat anything that her mother-in-law prepared for her. Then, tomorrow, she would get them all out of there as soon as she could, whether the house came through or not.

Brad and Andy reached her in a couple of minutes, and then they all walked toward the house together, hand-in-hand. Brad told them he was having the best Father's Day he'd ever had, and thanked them again for the picture.

"I'm the luckiest man on earth," he told them, happily, "with the best son and the best wife any man could hope for."

They had just reached the patio, and Andy had hurried over to Madeline to tell her about a school of porpoises they had seen, when Victoria's cell phone rang.

When the real estate agent told her their offer had been accepted, she squealed with excitement and cried out without thinking, "Brad, they accepted!" Realizing she shouldn't have blurted that out in front of Madeline, Victoria grimaced and stepped across the patio to finish her conversation with the agent. He told her they could move in immediately, renting the home until the closing was finalized.

After Victoria's outburst, Brad glanced sheepishly at his mother, who seemed to pick up on what they were talking about immediately. Even from across the patio, Victoria could see her mother-in-law's face fill with disgust. She fumed at Brad, "How could you?" and immediately went inside, slamming the sliding glass door behind her.

"Is Mimi mad at me?" Andy asked his father. "Did I do something?"

"No, son. Mimi's not mad at you. I just need to have a talk with your grandmother about something."

Victoria watched the drama as she spoke to the agent and quickly ended the call.

"Hey, Andy," she said, taking the boy's hand, "Do you want to watch the end of *Finding Nemo*? You never did get to see the end, did you?"

"Yay! *Finding Nemo*." He pulled her toward the door.

Brad mouthed "Thank you," to Victoria and headed into the house to find his mother while Victoria took Andy upstairs. When they arrived in the sitting room,

Victoria fast-forwarded about halfway through the movie.

"You may have seen part of this, but pretty soon new parts will come on," she told him.

"That's okay," Andy said, sitting down cross-legged in front of the television. "I don't mind watching part of it again."

Victoria saw a long confrontation coming with her mother-in-law, and she didn't want Andy to be any part of it.

When she was midway down the stairs, she heard raised voices coming from the kitchen. She stopped outside the door, listening to Brad and his mother in the middle of a heated argument.

"All I've ever tried to do my entire life is to make you happy," she heard Brad saying. "But nothing is ever enough."

"Please don't move, Bradley," Madeline pleaded. "I couldn't bear it if you and Andy left me."

"I don't want to move either, Mother. And we wouldn't be moving if you hadn't pulled that little prank with Andy's school. Everything was fine until then. Why did you do that, Mother? Why? Andy is capable of loving both you and Victoria. Why do you always let your jealousy get the best of you? "

"I didn't do anything," his mother insisted. "It was her, that woman you brought into this house. It's like she's cast a spell on Andrew. But she's not a good mother. She just gives him what he wants so he'll like her, and then when he really needs her, she doesn't even pick him up from school on time."

There was a pause. Victoria wanted to peek in the door to see what was happening, but she didn't dare. It was Brad's place to deal with his mother, not hers.

After a few moments of silence, Brad spoke. His voice had a steely resolve that she'd never heard from him when he spoke to his mother.

"Mother, I know you didn't have a dentist appointment that day."

"What?" She sounded shocked. "What are you talking about?"

"I called Dr. Jenkins' office. They told me that you didn't have a dentist appointment that day. You planned it all, didn't you? Just as Victoria said you did."

His mother's voice sounded enraged. "You were checking up on me? My own son doesn't believe me?"

"I didn't want to, but I had no other choice."

His mother didn't say anything for a long while and then said in a weepy voice, "I didn't want to tell you this, Bradley, but it wasn't the dentist I went to. It was a doctor, a specialist. I'm having some health problems. I just didn't want you to know."

Victoria rolled her eyes. "Oh c'mon!" she said to herself. "Please don't believe this bullshit, Brad. That woman is as healthy as a horse. She's just trying to get out of this."

But she wasn't really surprised when she heard Brad's concerned voice respond, "Oh no, Mother. What's wrong? I knew there had to be some explanation."

"Are you kidding me?" Victoria fumed internally as she listened to Madeline tell Brad about the "mystery ailment" that she was being tested for, one Victoria was certain would miraculously clear up when it was convenient for her mother-in-law. But she could tell that Brad was hanging on her every word.

Victoria couldn't listen to any more of this. Couldn't listen to her mother-in-law manufacture more lies to reel in Brad, to sabotage the only chance they'd had to move out of this house. She pushed open the door and entered the room.

"Please tell me you don't believe this garbage, Brad?"

Madeline jerked her head toward Victoria, surprised to hear her daughter-in-law's voice enter the conversation.

"Victoria!" Brad chided. "Don't be so insensitive. Mother is having health problems."

Victoria saw a shrewd smile playing with the corners of Madeline's lips. When Brad glanced at his mother, she cast her eyes toward him with a pitiful expression and grasped her throat as if she were deeply offended.

The performance incensed Victoria. "Brad, your mother is lying. It's so obvious."

Her mother-in-law's face took on a horrified expression as if she had been deeply wounded.

"Victoria!" Brad was in full defensive mode. "My mother is not a liar. She's sick."

"Brad, not only is your mother a liar, she's a compulsive liar—and maybe a lot more."

"Don't you talk about my poor mother that way. After everything she's been through in her life, and now she's dealing with this."

He stopped and seemed to gather his nerve. "Now is not the time for us to move, Victoria. I can't leave her now. We'll need to wait until we get Mother through this ordeal."

Victoria took one look at her mother-in-law's smug face and all the resentment and anger she'd been repressing for weeks came roaring to the surface.

"After what your mother has been through her whole life? Give me a break! Your mother wasn't in any orphanage in Austria. She came from a wealthy family and was such a rebellious, unmanageable teenager—and a compulsive liar—that they had to send her away to try to straighten her out."

Madeline's face flushed with rage. "That's not true! I've seen you talking to that crazy old busybody on the beach. He doesn't know anything about me or my life."

"Well, your husband told him plenty."

Brad looked back and forth between the two screaming women.

"Enough!" He held up his hands for silence. "What's this you're saying, Victoria?"

Victoria tried to compose herself, but she having trouble doing it.

"William said your father told him that your mother was not raised in an orphanage. That she lies about that to get sympathy from people. Most of all from you."

Brad frowned as he tried to absorb the information. "My father said that?"

Madeline reacted quickly. "Don't believe anything that gossipy old man says. He's just trying to cause trouble."

Brad seemed lost in thought. Finally, he said, "Dad and William were good friends. Dad always told me I could trust William."

Victoria piped up. "William has known this all these years, Brad, and has never told you because he didn't want to interfere in your relationship with your mother. He only told me because he knew how upset I was and thought we needed to get out of the house as soon as possible."

Madeline shook her head. "He needs to mind his own business."

Brad's face had a glazed look, as if he didn't know what to believe. "Mother, is it true? Did you grow up in an orphanage? Or have you been lying to me all these years?"

His mother took him by the hands and stared deeply into his eyes.

"Of course, it's true, Bradley. I'm your mother. I wouldn't lie to you."

Brad nodded his head and let out a long sigh. "I want to believe you, Mother. I don't know what I'd do if I thought you'd been lying to me about that all these years. That's part of the reason I've stayed. I thought you went through such an ordeal when you were a child that I didn't want to do anything that would cause you more pain."

She narrowed her eyes and gave him a knowing look. "I haven't been lying, Brad. Trust me."

Victoria could see that his mother was winning him over. She wanted to tell him about what William had said about his father's death, that his mother had poisoned him. But she couldn't bring herself to do it. She couldn't hurl an accusation like that without proof. And certainly not in front of his mother. God knows what she'd do if she found out William had told her that.

Watching the strange dynamic between mother and son, Victoria felt almost as disgusted with Brad as she did with his mother. How gullible could he be? She only hoped he would still move out with her tomorrow. But if he changed his mind and decided to stay home and nurse his mother through her fake illness, she was moving anyway.

"I need to think," Brad said, running his hands through his hair. "I need to think." He pushed away from the kitchen table, stood up, and strode out of the room. Victoria heard the sliding glass door in the living room slam shut as he went outside.

Left alone with each other, her mother-in-law put her hands on her hips and glared at Victoria with undisguised contempt. "I hope you're happy," she said. "You should be ashamed of yourself for telling a son lies about his mother."

Victoria shrugged. "I would be, if I were telling lies." Then she turned her back on her mother-in-law and left the kitchen.

Chapter Thirty-Three

Victoria ran immediately back upstairs to check on Andy and start packing. Regardless of what decision Brad made, Victoria was leaving first thing in the morning. She couldn't wait to get out of Madeline's house. She hoped she would be leaving with her husband and stepson, but if she wasn't, she would just have to learn to live with that.

Andy was happily engaged in watching the end of his movie. He barely noticed Victoria come in the room. She went directly into the bedroom and pushed the door closed between the sitting room and the master bedroom. She took a quick shower and changed into a pair of jeans and an old college T-shirt. She went immediately to the closet, pulled out her biggest suitcase, and went to work emptying her clothes out of the bureau drawers and into her suitcase.

When the first suitcase was crammed full, she took out another smaller piece of luggage and began to fill it with her shoes. She was down on her hands and knees in the closet packing her shoes when she suddenly became aware of the presence of someone else in the room. She froze.

"Mommy?"

"Oh, Andy. Thank goodness." She exhaled in relief.

"What are you doing?" he asked.

Victoria had hoped to be able to tell Andy that they were all moving together to a nice new home near the beach, where he would have his own playroom. But right now, she wasn't sure if Brad was coming with her or not.

She stood up and crossed the room to shut the door to the bedroom so no one could hear them. Then she sat down on the edge of the bed.

"Andy, come sit down next to me," she said, patting the bed. "I need to tell you something."

She waited until he sat down and gazed up at her with curiosity.

"Andy, Mommy is going away for a while. I'm going to move into a new house, and I hope Daddy decides that both of you are going to move in with me too."

Andy's face took on a worried little frown and tears started to fill his eyes.

"But why, Mommy? I want you to stay here."

"Well, of course, I want to stay here with you too, Andy, and I hope your Daddy decides for you and him to come with me. I won't be far away."

Worry lines creased his forehead. "But why can't we all stay here?"

Victoria hesitated and chose her words carefully. "Well, Andy, when you grow up, big people like to move away from their parents and get a house of their own. Not live with their mommies anymore."

"You mean Mimi?"

Victoria nodded. "That's right. When you grow up, you visit your mommy, but you don't live with her. Do you understand?"

Andy's face darkened. "Mimi's not going to like that."

"Well," Victoria said. "She'll get used to it. All mommies have to get used to it when their children grow up. Even grown-ups can't always have exactly what they want. I hope Daddy decides to move too so we can all be together, just in a different house. I think you and Daddy and I will all be together in our new house soon."

Tears began running down Andy's cheeks, and he started to become agitated.

He grabbed her hand. "No, Mommy. Please don't go."

She felt horrible that she'd had to tell him this way and that it was upsetting him so much. But she had to get out of this house, and get out quickly, especially after what William had just told her. She thought again about that soup.

"I don't want to go, Andy, but I have to. It's just hard for Mimi and me to live in the same house."

Andy was squeezing her hand so hard it felt like the circulation was cutting off. He peered up at her with terror-filled eyes. "That's what my other mommy said too."

Victoria's mouth went dry, and it felt like a steel glove was clutching her heart.

"What do you mean, Andy?"

He was crying harder now, grasping her hands with both of his. "She said the same thing right before she started riding her bicycle."

Victoria caught her breath, a terrible fear starting to take over her body.

He looked up at her in horror and his voice rose an octave. "You're not going to ride a bicycle are you?"

She put her arm around him and pulled him close. His little body was shaking. She realized hers was too.

"No, Andy. Don't worry. I'm not going to ride a bicycle."

"Good. Please don't ride a bicycle, Mommy."

Victoria remembered something that Brad had wondered about.

"Andy," she asked. "Who told you your other mommy was riding a bicycle when a car hit her?"

Andy blinked as if he didn't understand the question. Then he said, "Nobody told me."

Victoria was confused. "Then how do you know? Did you hear somebody talking about it?"

He dried his eyes with his hand and stared up at her innocently. He shook his head.

"Then how?" Victoria asked.

Tears began streaming down his face as he stared up at her. Finally he said, "I saw her when the car banged. I was in my car seat and saw her out the window."

Victoria's hands flew up to her mouth, and she felt like she couldn't breathe. Andy was in the car when Erica was run over.

"Andy, I have a very important question to ask you. And I want you to think real hard and be absolutely sure when you answer me. Do you understand?"

Andy nodded, a serious expression on his face.

"Do you remember who was driving the car that day when your other mommy got hurt on the bicycle?"

Andy peered up at her and nodded.

"Will you tell me who it was, Andy?"

He nodded and murmured in a voice so low she almost didn't hear him, "Mimi."

Chapter Thirty-Four

Victoria screamed internally, "Oh my God. Oh my God. Oh my God!" She wanted to race from the room, run down the stairs, jump in her car, and never come back.

She inhaled a deep breath of air and stared down at Andy. They had to get out of the house, and they had to get out right now.

She glanced around the room and quickly tossed as many essentials as she could fit into the smaller suitcase and clicked it shut. Grabbing a handful of clothes from her closet, still on hangers, she threw them over her arm and took hold of the handles of both suitcases and pulled them toward the door.

"C'mon, Andy. Let's go. Do you think you could carry that little shoulder bag for me?"

Andy nodded confidently. "I can carry it. It's not too heavy for me."

Loaded down, Victoria asked Andy to open the door to the bedroom. Then she told him to wait as she peeked outside. Where was her mother-in-law? The house was quiet. Brad must still be out on the beach.

Putting her finger to her lips to signal Andy to move quietly, she tiptoed out of the room toward the staircase. Something morbid in her couldn't keep her from glancing over the rail, at the long drop down to the tile floor below. It wouldn't surprise her at all if her mother-in-law had pushed Brad's first wife off this railing too.

She glanced around again, half expecting her mother-in-law to leap out at her from the shadows. Andy peered up at her, a questioning look on his face.

"Okay," she whispered. "Let's go downstairs."

Her hand trembling as she reached out to the banister, she readjusted the suitcases so that she could pull both of them with one hand. She wanted to run down the stairs, but she knew the noise would alert Brad's mother. Instead, she forced herself to move slowly, one step at a time, as quietly as she could.

When they reached the bottom, she pulled the suitcases quickly to the front door and had just opened it, when she saw a quick flash of movement beside her.

The sound of her mother-in-law's voice sent a jolt of fear through her body. She screamed and jerked her head to the side to see Madeline standing a few feet away from her holding Andy in front of her by his shoulders.

"You can go. Good riddance. But Andrew stays." Her voice was as clipped and cold as Victoria had ever heard it.

"Brad!" Victoria yelled out. But there was no answer. He must still be out on the beach.

Victoria pushed her bags outside the door and motioned to Andy. "C'mon, Andy. Come with me."

Andy looked up at his grandmother as if he wasn't sure what to do. She tightened her grip on his shoulders.

"I said go!" her mother-in-law shouted at her. "Andrew stays here."

Victoria wasn't sure what to do. She didn't want to leave the boy, but what was she supposed to do? Try to wrestle him from the grips of his murderous grandmother? She needed to find Brad. She couldn't do anything now on her own, and she knew Madeline wouldn't hurt Andy. For all her many faults, Brad's mother loved that little boy. Maybe too much.

"Daddy and I will be back, Andy. Don't you worry." With one last look at her stepson, she pulled the door shut behind her.

She raced across the driveway to her car, threw her luggage and her purse into the trunk, and tucked her car keys into the back pocket of her jeans. She slammed down the lid, and momentarily thought about jumping into the driver's seat and escaping this horrible house forever. She'd like nothing more than to put this whole frightening chapter of her life in her rear-view mirror.

But she knew she couldn't do that. She loved her husband, and she loved her stepson far too much to run away, to not stay and fight for them. They all had to get away from that fiendish woman. If she had killed her husband and run over Brad's wife, Erica, what else might she be capable of?

Victoria ran around the side of the house and down the narrow dirt pathway that led to the beach. When she reached the sand, she looked frantically in both directions, but didn't see Brad anywhere. It was starting to get dark, and huge gray clouds had rolled in, blocking out any light from the setting sun. Long, dark shadows covered the beach, making visibility difficult.

She ran toward the north first, squinting into the distance, but there was no sign of him. So she turned around and ran back in the other direction. When she was almost to their house again, she saw Brad coming out onto the beach from the back of William's house. So that's where he's been, talking to William, Victoria said to herself.

Brad was walking at a determined pace toward the house. By the time she reached him, he was at the house next door to theirs and moving at such a fast pace that she couldn't keep up with him.

"Brad, stop. Brad, please stop. I have to tell you something."

"Not now, Victoria," he said, not slowing down. She had never seen him like this. He was moving like a locomotive train racing out of control.

"Brad, please, slow down. It's important. It's something about Erica's death. I have to tell you."

"What about it?" he said, unlatching the gate to the patio.

She grabbed his arm, forcing him to stop. "Brad, your mother did it. She's the one who ran her down. Andy was in the backseat when she did it. He just told me."

Brad stopped and stared at her in horror. "Oh my God. She did that too?" He added, his voice filled with pain. "And with Andy in the car?"

Victoria nodded. "And, Brad," she said. "She probably killed Marie too."

In a rage, he flew across the patio and slammed open the sliding glass door.

"Mother!" he screamed. "Get down here!"

Chapter Thirty-Five

Brad's mother appeared at the top of the staircase. She stood still, glaring down them at down, a haughty expression on her face. Victoria wasn't sure if she was going to come down the stairs or not. Finally, she plunged her hands into the pockets of her black slacks, lifted her head, and slowly descended the staircase, almost regally, like a queen giving an audience to her subjects.

When she reached the bottom, she took a few steps into the living room, stopped, and stared at them. Waiting. Brad stepped toward her, while Victoria hung back by the door.

"Where's Andy?" he asked sharply.

"Upstairs. Asleep."

Brad nodded and clenched his jaw.

"How could you, Mother? How could you do it?"

"Do what?" she asked, frowning. "I don't know what you're talking about."

"You killed my father."

Madeline laughed tightly. "I did no such thing. You've been talking to that crazy old busybody again, haven't you? Him and his ridiculous theories. Nobody believes him."

"They're not so ridiculous. I always knew something wasn't right. I heard you and Dad arguing before I went to summer camp. I could tell Dad wasn't happy."

She rolled her eyes and said derisively, "Your father. Nothing ever made him happy."

"He was so young, so healthy. There's no way he had a heart attack."

She shrugged. "It happens. He didn't eat right, and he drank too much."

"You poisoned him, Mother. I know you did. Just like William said. He said the police thought so too. They just couldn't prove it."

She sighed and shook her head. "I did not poison your father, Bradley."

"Is that why you wouldn't let me come to the funeral? Because the police were investigating? You made me stay at camp. I never even got to say goodbye.

By the time I got home, he'd been buried, and it was like he never existed."

She looked away and shrugged, as it if wasn't important. "At your age, I thought it would be too much for you."

Brad clenched his fists, his face growing a deeper shade of red. He glanced back at Victoria and then turned to face his mother again.

"And now I find out that it was you who ran down Erica."

His mother took a sharp intake of breath, obviously shocked by the statement.

"What are you talking about? I did no such thing."

Brad roared at her, "Stop lying! All you do is lie. About growing up in an orphanage. About poisoning my father. About running over Erica. Just stop!"

His mother raised her chin and denied his accusations again. "I did none of those things."

Victoria hung in the background, not saying a word. This battle was between Brad and his mother.

Brad wasn't holding back. "You can deny it all you want, Mother, but I'm done. I'm taking Andy, and we're getting out of here."

His mother stepped forward ominously. "You can leave, but you're not taking Andrew. He's staying here with me."

Brad stared at his mother as if she'd lost her mind. "Andy is my son. Of course, he's coming with me."

"Andrew's not going with you." Her face was like stone. "You're both terrible parents. He will be much better off with me. I like being a mother, and I'm good at it. Not like her." She threw a nasty glance at Victoria.

"Mother, don't be ridiculous. Get out of the way."

When he moved sideways to go around her, she stepped into his path.

"Bradley," she said in a taunting voice, "aren't you forgetting something?"

He stopped cold and didn't answer.

A shrewd smile crossed his mother's lips.

Victoria couldn't help but ask, "What? What is it?"

Madeline narrowed her eyes and glanced at Victoria. "Do you want to tell her, Bradley? Or shall I?"

Brad glared at his mother, as if daring her to speak.

But Madeline clearly was enjoying this. "I'm sure it's seemed strange to you, Victoria that Bradley has always so adamantly refused to leave this house."

Madeline's mouth twisted into a smile and she mused, "Of course, he's a Reynolds, and this is where he should be. And his son deserves to be raised with the same outstanding upbringing Bradley received. And who better to provide that than me. But there have been a few times when Bradley has needed more persuading."

She gave her son a piercing look. "So, we've had our little secret, haven't we, Bradley dear?"

"You shut up about that!"

Victoria had never heard Brad scream at anyone that way.

"What Brad is trying to tell you, Victoria, is—"

"Stop, Mother!" Brad looked across the room at Victoria, a guilty expression covering his face.

He stared at the floor, unable to meet her eyes. Victoria wondered if he were going to say anything or not.

Finally, he blurted out, "Mother didn't kill Marie. I did."

Chapter Thirty-Six

Victoria stared at him in disbelief and immediately started edging toward the door. Wild with fear, she glanced out the window, searching for a way to escape. It was a pitch black moonless night, but better to be alone in the dark than standing here in a room with two murderers.

Brad noticed her movement toward the door and yelled out to her. "No, please wait, Victoria. Let me explain."

She had her hand on the doorknob.

"Let her go, Bradley," his mother interjected. "She's no good for you or Andrew."

Brad whirled around at her. "Shut up, Mother!"

Madeline pursed her lips into a grim line and sent Brad a piercing look.

"Victoria," Brad pleaded. "Let me explain. Please."

Tears in her eyes, Victoria continued to clutch the doorknob. But she waited. She couldn't help herself. She wanted to hear what he had to say.

"It's true. It's my fault Marie died. But I didn't mean to kill her."

He paused as if he were trying to figure out how to say it. "She was beside herself," he began. "She wanted to move, to move away from this house. We'd lived here the whole time we were married. We were so young, and she seemed to love it. She loved living on the beach. But after Andy was born, things changed. She said Mother was trying to take over the baby. Was making her feel like she wasn't a good mother." He fired a nasty look at his mother. She met his gaze.

"I was just trying to calm her down, to make her listen to reason. She said she was leaving. She'd packed her things, Andy's things. I grabbed her by the arms to talk to her. She started to struggle. Then she… then she… lost her balance." He stared over at the spot on the foyer where her body had landed.

Victoria didn't know what to think. His story had such a ring of truth to it, especially the part about Madeline trying to take over the baby. Still, his wife had died, and died because her husband couldn't stand up to his mother. Poor Marie.

"You have to believe me, Victoria," Brad pleaded. "It's the God's honest truth."

She took a step away from him.

"Well, then why lie about it?" she asked. "It sounds like it was an accident. Why tell everyone it was suicide?"

He glared at his mother. She returned it, evenly more intensely.

"Mother saw it all. She said I would be charged with manslaughter, maybe worse. That I would go to prison. The thought of prison—I just couldn't take that. She said it would be easier all the way around if we just said it was suicide. Marie had been having some issues with post-partum depression, though she was getting over it. But we knew the doctor would back us up on that."

Victoria felt nauseous. This sick mother-son relationship had caused the deaths of two women. She was determined she was not going to be third. She turned the doorknob.

"I'm sorry, Brad. I'm sorry for what's happened to you. But this is all too much for me. I'm leaving."

His mother flashed him a triumphant look, but Brad crossed the room quickly and grabbed Victoria by the arms.

"No, Victoria, no. Please don't leave me. We'll face this together. We'll get Andy and go. Whatever you want. Just please don't leave me."

Victoria wanted to break away and run, but when he said Andy's name, all she could think of was getting that sweet little boy out of there. She couldn't let him be raised by a murderess.

She paused for a long moment before she answered. "Okay, Brad. Let's get Andy and go. But I'm not saying I'll stay with you. I just want to get Andy out of here."

Brad's face lit up. "You don't have to promise me, Victoria. I'll win you back. I'll do whatever it takes to win you back. C'mon," he said, taking her hand. "Let's go get Andy."

But when he turned around, his mother reached into her pocket and pulled out a gun. She pointed it at Victoria.

"I told you," Madeline said, her eyes flashing anger, "Andrew is staying with me."

Stunned, Victoria shrank behind Brad, who stepped in front of her to protect her. "Mother, for God's sake, put the gun down."

"It's her or me, Bradley," Madeline said. "Who do you choose? The three of us can keep living here just as we always have. But don't try to take Andrew from me. I've raised him. Do you think that because you're married again you can just throw me away, like I'm some piece of garbage? That's not going to happen."

Brad shook his head. "Mother, you know how much I've appreciated everything you've done for Andy. But you're Andy's grandmother, not his mother. Why couldn't you just accept that?"

She acted like she hadn't heard him and shifted her position to get a better shot at Victoria. "All we have to do is get rid of her. She's the problem. No one will know. We'll tell people she moved back to California. She doesn't have any relatives. No one will ever know."

Victoria cowered behind Brad, trying to shrink even smaller behind his back.

"Mother, don't talk that way. Put down the gun. Victoria is my wife, and I love her. I would never do anything to harm her."

Madeline continued to move around, leveling the gun so she could take aim at Victoria. "This one's worse than the last one."

Brad narrowed his eyes at her. "Are you talking about Erica? How could do that, Mother? Run over my wife for God's sake? I never in my wildest dreams would ever have thought you were capable of something like that. I thought you and Andy were up in Savannah that day visiting some friend of yours."

Madeline lifted her chin and smiled. "I did go to Savannah, but I took care of the Erica problem before I left. And then, I got the car fixed up in Georgia. That bike made quite a mess of my fender."

His face contorted in disgust. "And you did it with Andy in the backseat."

She gave him a surprised look. "Well, what was I supposed to do? Leave him at home by himself? What kind of a parent do you think I am?"

He stared at his mother as if he were seeing her for the first time. "How could you do that? And how could you kill Erica?"

"Because she was leading you around by the nose just like this one is. Trying to make you leave your home, to take Andrew with you and leave me alone."

Growing angrier, Madeline snarled at Brad, "You are so weak. Such a disappointment. Why couldn't you be a man and stand up to them and tell them you were going to live where you wanted to live?"

"They weren't leading me anywhere, Mother. I wanted to go. I wanted to move. Away from this house. Away from you."

His mother became enraged. "Don't you talk to me that way! Your father tried that once and look what happened to him."

Brad narrowed his eyes at her. "What about my father? What did you do to my father?"

She waved the barrel of the gun at him. "Oh, you're always so concerned about your saintly father. You put him on such a pedestal. Your father who flirted with anything in a skirt."

Brad face turned bright red. Victoria had never seen him so angry. "Don't you talk about my father that way!"

"You want to know about your father, Bradley? When I got back from dropping you off at summer camp, I came home to find your father in bed with another woman. In *my* bed! Then he tells me he wants a divorce. And, on top of that, he wants me to move out of the house. *Me!* Says this is his family home, and it should stay in his family." She paused and a triumphant tone entered her voice. "Well, that wasn't going to happen."

Brad stared at her coldly. "So you killed him? You poisoned him?"

"Well, what else was I supposed to do? I wasn't moving out of my house," she shrieked. "He needed to be punished. No one treats me like that."

Madeline waved the gun at Brad again. "Get out of the way, Brad. We'll get rid of her and then everything will be fine again. You'll see."

Overcome with panic, Victoria slid to the ground behind him, folding her arms over her head to try to protect herself.

Without warning, Brad dove for the gun. He and his mother began struggling wildly for it and fell to the floor, both trying to grab it away from each other. Victoria cowered against the wall, too terrified to move. Suddenly, a shot exploded out of the cylinder, and the gun flew from their hands and skidded across the floor.

Victoria scurried across the room to pick it up. Brad and his mother lay toppled in a heap, neither of them moving. She couldn't tell if one of them had been hit or not. But then, Brad's mother pushed away from her son, crawled onto her knees, and stood up. She stared first at

Victoria, and then at the gun she held limply in her hand. The next thing Victoria knew, Madeline ran across the living room and raced up the stairs.

Victoria went quickly to Brad, rolled him over, and screamed when she saw blood pouring out of his chest. She cradled his head in her lap.

"Brad. Oh, Brad," she cried, caressing his hair.

He struggled to open his eyes.

"I'm so sorry, honey," he said, gasping for air. "I'm so sorry for bringing you into this."

Tears streamed down her face. "Don't try to talk, baby. I'm going to call an ambulance. They'll be here soon, and everything will be okay." As she glanced around desperately for her phone, she realized it was in her purse, locked in the car. And Brad was dressed in his swim trunks, so he didn't have his phone with him either.

"I don't have a phone!" she cried frantically.

Brad tried to smile, but as he did, blood ran out of the corner of his mouth, down his chin.

"It's not going to help, anyway," he choked, staring up at her. "I love you, Victoria. You're the love of my life. You really are."

Victoria's heart was breaking. "You're the love of my life too, Brad."

A little sparkle came into his eyes as he said, "We had fun, didn't we?"

She leaned down and kissed his forehead.

"So much fun."

He squeezed her hand and his voice faded. "Take care of Andy."

"I will."

Then Brad closed his eyes and was gone.

Chapter Thirty-Seven

Clutching him to her chest, sobbing, Victoria couldn't believe her husband was dead. Her sweet Brad. The love of her life. It felt as if all the life had drained out of her too. She slid him back down onto the floor and curled up next to him, holding him, not caring as his blood seeped onto her clothing, over her bare arms. She didn't know how long she lay there, next to him—her mind seemed to have stop functioning. And except for a pounding, pounding, pounding at the front of her brain, the world had ceased to exist.

She replayed the last words they spoke to each other over and over in her mind, until the words began to take meaning. *Take care of Andy. Take care of Andy.* She sat up and looked around. The gun was on the floor by Brad's foot. She struggled to her feet and picked it up.

Holding it in front of her with both hands, she started to climb the stairs. She had to find Andy.

When she reached the second floor landing, she looked down over the railing and pictured Marie's delicate body lying in a heap on the tile below. The horror of it was too much to imagine. Shaking the image from her brain, she started to move slowly down the darkened hallway toward Andy's bedroom, listening for sounds, looking for movement. Her mother-in-law was here somewhere—waiting for her.

The entire wing was dark, and Victoria wasn't familiar enough with this part of the house to know where the light switches were. When she reached Andy's room, she tiptoed to the door, felt around on the wall until she located the light switch, and then leveled the gun in front of her.

When she flipped on the light, she jumped back out of the doorway, expecting her mother-in-law to leap out at her. But nothing happened. Nothing came from the room except silence. Slowly, she peered around the door jamb toward Andy's bed. He wasn't there. Carefully entering his bedroom, she kept the gun in front of her, searching all corners of the room for her stepson. She counted on the element of surprise as she jerked open the closet door. But no one was there. Before leaving the room, she checked under the bed, too, but no Andy.

Despite a crushing fear, Victoria continued, determined to find her stepson. Moving slowly down the dimly lit hallway, brightened by the light from Andy's room, Victoria stepped slowly toward her mother-in-law's bedroom.

When she turned a corner, the hallway became almost totally black again. She couldn't remember exactly how far down the hallway Madeline's bedroom was. She'd only been there once and remembered that it was in the farthest corner of the house. It was a huge room, that much she knew, even bigger than their master suite. Instead of having a separate sitting room, her room had a loveseat, two armchairs, and a coffee table set off to the side as you entered the room. She remembered a beautiful Tiffany lamp that sat on an end table by the door. At the back of the room was a connected bathroom, as well as a large walk-in closet.

Her hands trembling, she felt her way along the wall until she realized she had reached the door to her mother-in-law's bedroom. She thought it would be closed and probably locked. But the door was open. As she peered into the darkness of the bedroom, she saw the faintest sliver of light shining through the crack of the bathroom door in the far corner of the room. She reached her hand inside the room to feel for the light switch, ready to jump back when the light flashed on. But she couldn't find a switch. She remembered the Tiffany lamp by the armchair and started moving to her left to turn it on.

Out of nowhere, she felt a searing pain in her right arm as sharp steel dug into her flesh. The gun flew out of her hand and slid across the floor as her mother-in-law's frenzied face became illuminated by a light under her chin. Victoria shrieked at the haunting, ghostly sight. She immediately realized the light was coming from a cell phone that her mother grasped in one hand. In the other, she held a bloody pair of scissors in a threatening stance aimed at Victoria's throat.

Her arm throbbing with pain, Victoria heard her mother-in-law punch three keys. "911" the voice on the phone answered. "What is your emergency?"

"Help me, help me. Please," her mother-in-law screamed. "This is Madeline Reynolds. My daughter-in-law has gone crazy and shot my son. She's trying to kill me. Help me. Hurry!"

Madeline clicked off the phone, but the light from the cell phone continued to illuminate her face. That smug smile that Victoria had come to hate so much was back on her mother-in-law's face.

"Thought you were going to just waltz in here and steal my family, didn't you?" Madeline raised the scissors and moved her face so close to Victoria's that she could feel her breath on her cheek. Trying to step backward, Victoria's back hit the wall.

"I never wanted to steal your family, Madeline," Victoria cried, putting her hands in front of her defensively. "I just wanted to be part of it. To be Brad's wife and Andy's mother—and your daughter-in-law."

"You'll never be Andrew's mother. You'll never be anybody's mother." She raised her arm above her head, ready to plunge the scissors into Victoria's chest.

Victoria leaned to her side, groping with her left hand to grab anything she could find to protect herself. Her fingers hit something glass. She realized it was the Tiffany lamp. Swiftly, she stretched her arm farther, grasped the base of the lamp, and swung it out at her mother-in-law. Glass shattered and her mother-in-law groaned and fell against the wall.

Victoria raced out of the room, down the darkened hallway, past Andy's room to the staircase. She heard a noise behind her in the distance. She kept running, but chanced taking a quick glance over her shoulder. Her mother-in-law was chasing her, the scissors raised in the air.

Chapter Thirty-Eight

"You should have eaten your soup, Victoria," Madeline shouted from behind. "It would have made everything so much easier."

Victoria cringed as she realized her suspicions were true, that her mother-in-law had served her poisoned soup. But she didn't stop running down the stairs. She grabbed at her back pocket for her car keys but couldn't feel them. She patted down her other back pocket. Her keys weren't there. What could have happened to them?

All she could think of was that they must have fallen out of her pocket in the living room. When she reached the bottom of the stairs, she looked quickly behind her. Madeline was at the top of the staircase. Victoria hurried across the living room, feeling nausea rise in her stomach as she saw Brad's body, covered in blood, sprawled across the floor.

She tried not to look at him, instead concentrating on finding her keys. Then she saw them, lying next to the wall near the end table. But when she looked back, Madeline was already at the bottom of the stairs, running across the living room at her. With no time to retrieve the keys, Victoria jerked open the sliding glass door and ran outside onto the patio.

As she raced around the pool and unlatched the gate, she heard a primal wail come from the living room. Turning to look back through the open door, she saw Madeline standing over Brad's body.

"You killed my son. If it weren't for you, my son would still be alive," her mother-in-law raged as she stepped through the sliding glass door to the patio. "You're going to pay for this."

Victoria raced down the path, thankful that at least that she was wearing tennis shoes. When she reached the sand, she wasn't sure if she should run north or south. She considered running to William's house, but she didn't want to put him or his wife in danger. After what William had told Brad, there was no telling what Madeline would do to him if she saw him.

The Mother-in-Law

The cloud cover was so thick that the only light on the beach was from a few homes with deck lights several hundred feet down the beach. Victoria knew she could never reach them before Madeline caught up with her. Her mother-in-law was a marathon runner. Victoria probably couldn't even run around the block without collapsing.

Still, she kept running, crossing over the soft sand to run along the hard-packed sand of the shoreline. She looked back over her shoulder, but the cloud cover made it so dark that she couldn't see a foot in front of her. When waves weren't crashing on the shore, though, she could hear the steady jogging pace of Madeline's steps not far behind her.

Victoria knew it was only a matter of time before her mother-in-law caught up with her. She couldn't outrun her. But the inky darkness gave her an idea. She moved closer to the shoreline and just as a huge wave broke, she squatted down in the shadows of the moving water. Then she waited silently until she heard Madeline run past her.

Her arm ached from the pain of the stab, and when the salt water splashed on it, the wound burned so much that she almost screamed out. But she managed to remain quiet and still until her mother-in-law had run a good distance past. Soaked from the waist down, Victoria then started running back toward the house. She just needed to grab her car keys and get out of there. Since her mother-in-law had called 911, the police were on their way, but they'd never arrive in enough time to save her. It was nearly a half an hour drive to their remote beach location.

The clouds shifted and a few glimmers of light came down from the heavens, lighting up the beach. "Oh, God. Not now," Victoria begged, as she drew closer to the house. Her wet jeans and tennis shoes were slowing her down, but she only had about a hundred feet to go until she reached the path up to the house.

Suddenly, Victoria heard footsteps closing in on her from behind. She turned around to see a streak of silver coming at her and instinctively threw her good arm up in the air to block it. Pain seared through her wrist as the blade sunk in, but she managed to grab hold of Madeline's arm and pull her down. They tumbled into the sand, fighting for the scissors. Victoria felt the blade dig into her arms two more times as they fought. Somehow, she managed to climb on top of Madeline, her knees holding the older woman down as they both reached up in a fight for the scissors.

All of a sudden, bright lights blinded their eyes, and a man's voice yelled out, "Police. Drop the weapon!"

"Help! Get her off me," Madeline cried. "She's trying to kill me."

Two other police officers approached them with guns drawn. One of them said, "He said 'Drop the weapon.'"

Both Victoria and Madeline let go at the same time, and the scissors fell into the sand. A policewoman took Victoria by the shoulders and pulled her off her mother-in-law.

"Thank God you got here," Madeline said breathlessly as she stood up. She pointed at Victoria. "That woman shot my son and was trying to kill me."

"No, no," Victoria cried. "She shot Brad. And she chased me down the beach, trying to stab me with those scissors. Look at all the cuts I have."

Victoria held up her arms, which were covered in blood. Her T-shirt was also stained with blood. Brad's blood.

"I was just defending myself," Madeline insisted.

The police officers stared at Victoria suspiciously, frisked them both, and led them inside, past Brad's body.

Crime technicians were already working on the crime scene.

Brad's mother immediately collapsed next to the body. "My baby, my baby," she cried, reaching out to touch Brad's body. Then she pointed her finger at Victoria. "That woman did this."

A policewoman placed her hands under Madeline's arms and lifted her to her feet. "Are you sure he's gone?" Madeline asked the officer tearfully. "Are you sure he's not still alive?"

"Yes, ma'am. I'm sorry, but I'm afraid he's deceased," the policewoman told her. "You can't be here. Please come and sit down at the table."

Madeline was seated on the opposite end of the dining room table from Victoria. A police officer stood behind each one of them. A paramedic came over and started tending to the wounds on her arms. Victoria had begun weeping too when she saw Brad's body again, but she dried her eyes as her mother-in-law began making allegations against her to the police. As Madeline continued to sob, Victoria couldn't help but wonder how upset she really was about her son's death. Was all this emotion out of love, guilt, or just a show for the police?

A tall, balding man who appeared to be in his late fifties seemed to be in charge. His name was Detective Crandall. Victoria told him frantically, "My stepson is missing. She's done something with him. Please go find him."

The detective sent three uniformed officers to search the house. While they were gone, her mother-in-law managed to get her crying under control and asked for some tissues. With reddened eyes, she continued to glare across the table at Victoria, hurling out more accusations as the mood hit her.

Ten minutes later, one of the policemen came down the staircase, carrying Andy's limp body in his arms.

"Oh no!" Victoria cried out, starting to run across the room. "Is he alive?"

The policewoman grabbed her by the shoulders to hold her back as the officer carrying the child walked to the couch and lay him down on it. Andy wasn't moving.

Paramedics immediately started examining the boy. Victoria couldn't breathe. She felt as if she were hyperventilating. What had Madeline done to Andy? She felt like leaping across the table and choking her. Her mother-in-law seemed unconcerned and sat silently, uncharacteristically not saying a word as Andy was examined.

"He's breathing, but he won't wake up," one of the paramedics told them. "It looks like maybe he was drugged with something."

After a few minutes, the paramedics announced that all of his vital signs were fine, and that he seemed to have been drugged. They said they were taking him to the hospital for more tests.

"How could you do that?" Victoria screamed at her mother-in-law. "Drug your own grandson?"

Madeline ignored her and asked if she could have a glass of water.

Victoria wanted to know where Andy was found. The policeman said the boy was in the closet of the large bedroom, hidden way back in the corner under a quilt and some clothing.

Puzzled, Victoria wondered to herself, "In a closet, in the corner? Hidden by a quilt? What in the world was she going to do with him?"

That question was answered a few minutes later when another policeman who had been on the hunt for Andy came downstairs carrying two evidence bags. One contained the gun, but the other held two passports. The officer said he found them on the end table next to the bed along with a printout of airlines tickets to Austria—dated for tomorrow. One was in the name of Madeline Reynolds, the other in the name of Andrew Reynolds.

"I can't believe it," Victoria said. "She was going to steal him away to another country."

The detective glanced at the passports and waved the bag in front of Madeline. "Getting ready to take a little trip were you, Mrs. Reynolds?"

She ignored the question. "You'll find my daughter-in-law's fingerprints on that gun," she said triumphantly. "Not mine."

"Did you touch the gun?" he asked Madeline.

"Absolutely not."

Victoria protested. "But I only picked up the gun after she pointed it at us, and Brad tried to take it away from her. That's when it went off."

"If that's the case," the detective said, "forensics will show that. There will still be some of her prints on the gun as well."

Madeline became very quiet. "Well," she reminded him. "It is my gun. I have it for protection. So, undoubtedly, some of my fingerprints would be on it."

"But," the detective said, "if you didn't touch the gun today, there is one thing that absolutely would not be present. Gun powder residue on your hands."

He waved over one of the technicians. "Ladies, this officer will be doing a test for gunshot residue on each of you."

Madeline either had a really good poker face, or she had scrubbed her hands free of any gunshot residue, because she didn't seem concerned at all about the test. In fact, she smiled and gave Victoria a superior look.

"Well, I was holding the gun," Victoria said. "But not when it went off."

Her mother-in-law acted as if she had just realized something and said to the detective, "Well, I may have a little on my hands. I touched her hands when I was trying to stop her from killing me."

"That should show up in the residue test," the detective said. "There would be considerably more residue on the person who actually pulled the trigger."

Victoria noticed worry lines appear for the first time on her mother-in-law's forehead. Madeline seemed to think for a minute and then said to the detective. "I'm so glad you got my 911 call. I thought she was going to kill me."

The detective frowned at her. "Actually, ma'am, that call didn't come in until we were halfway here. It takes us quite a while to get way out here from the station."

Victoria was confused. "Then why were you coming here before that?"

"We received a call from one of your neighbors. A Mr. William Delaney. He said he heard a gunshot and was concerned because he feared there might trouble in the Reynolds house tonight. We've actually heard from Mr. Delaney a few times before."

Madeline pursed her lips. "You certainly don't believe that crazy old busybody do you?"

"What he says makes a lot of sense," the detective said, eyeing her with interest.

Victoria and her mother-in-law both submitted to the residue test. When it was over and the technician had completed the test, he walked over to the detective and whispered something in his ear.

Detective Crandall raised his eyebrows and smiled knowingly. "Aaah," he said. "Music to my ears."

He waved two officers over and pointed at Madeline. They walked over to stand behind her. "Mrs. Reynolds, would you please stand up."

Madeline frowned suspiciously and slowly stood up.

"Madeline Reynolds, you are under arrest for the murder of Bradley Reynolds. And don't be surprised if other charges will be forthcoming."

"But I didn't do it. She did it," Madeline protested, nodding her head toward Victoria as the officers handcuffed her hands behind her back. "I called 911 to report her. You have it on tape."

The detective chuckled. "It might surprise you to learn, Mrs. Reynolds, that your little ruse has been used by many a perpetrator to shift blame onto someone else."

Overcome with relief, Victoria stared in disbelief as her mother-in-law was handcuffed. Was it really over?

Madeline continued to protest as they started to lead her away. "But you have no proof. I'm just a poor grandmother, trying to take care of my family."

Detective Crandall's lips flattened into a grim line, and he shook his head in disgust.

"We've had our eye on you for a long time, Mrs. Reynolds. Years. We've just never had quite enough to arrest you."

Then he added, "And you know what the strange thing is, Mrs. Reynolds? It seems like just about everyone who lives in this house ends up dead. Everyone except you, that is."

Epilogue

Victoria sat up in bed and screamed. The face was there again. That hate-filled stare from the photograph of her mother-in-law standing at the window, watching her, Brad, and Andy on the beach.

It had been nearly two years, and the nightmares still came. Sometimes her mother-in-law was in the courtroom. Other times behind bars. And most frightening of all, chasing her down the beach.

Victoria had flown back to Florida from San Diego to testify, facing that horrible woman's piercing eyes across the courtroom. It had been hard on her, but in the end, worth it.

They finally got her. Guilty of poisoning her husband. Guilty of shooting her son. When her husband's remains were exhumed, they discovered he had indeed been murdered by a rare poison they had missed in their investigation twenty years before. A child psychologist interviewed Andy and determined with certainty that he was in the car when Erica Reynolds was run over on her bicycle by his grandmother. But because of lack of evidence, and to spare the child the ordeal of testifying, no charges were brought in that case.

Madeline was sentenced to life in prison, without the possibility of parole. She was still appealing her conviction. Her precious house had to be sold to pay her massive legal fees.

Victoria knew this latest nightmare wouldn't be her last. She took a deep breath, rolled over on her side, and closed her eyes. She'd try to fall back asleep, but she knew sleep wouldn't come easily. The cool ocean breeze coming in the window of their small bungalow near the Pacific might help. At least she didn't have to go to work tomorrow. The insurance money had allowed her to become a full-time mom to Andy until he was a little older.

Quiet footsteps entered the room, and she felt a little hand take hers.

"Mommy?

She glanced over to see Andy standing barefoot next to her bed in his Power Rangers pajamas. His blond cocker spaniel puppy, Dory, was by his side.

"Yes, Andy?"

"Did you have another bad dream?"

"I did, Andy. I'm sorry I woke you up."

"It's okay. Mommy, are we going to the zoo tomorrow?"

Victoria smiled at her son. "Yes, Andy. We're going to the zoo. Again."

"I'd like to go to the zoo every day if we could," he said excitedly. "I can't wait."

"Me either."

She opened her arms for a hug. "I love you, Andy. I'm the luckiest mommy in the whole world."

"I love you too, Mommy," he said, hugging her back.

He gave her a kiss on the cheek and started toward the door to go back to bed, patting his leg for the dog to follow.

"Mommy," he said, stopping to look back.

"Yes, Andy?"

"This time when you fall asleep, try to dream about Daddy in heaven. That will make you feel better."

Victoria glanced at the framed photograph on her nightstand of Andy sitting on his father's shoulders flying the kite, their Father's Day gift to Brad.

She smiled at her son. "You know what, Andy? That's a great idea. That's exactly what I'm going to do."

About the Author

A lifelong resident of Florida, Judy Moore writes primarily mysteries and thrillers, as well as lighter family fiction. A longtime news writer, editor, and magazine feature writer, she has a master's degree in journalism and was a college journalism professor. She has written two other mystery novels, *Murder in Vail,* set on the ski slopes of Colorado, and the golf mystery *Somebody Killed the Cart Girl,* set at a New England country club. Her Christmas anthology, *Christmas Interrupted,* contains three popular holiday novellas: *Airport Christmas, The Holiday House Sitter,* and *The Hitchhiker on Christmas Eve.* An earlier novella, *Birds of Prey,* and a new novelette, *Football Blues,* are also available on Amazon. Visit Judy Moore online at https://www.amazon.com/Judy-Moore/e/B007WTTGPM.

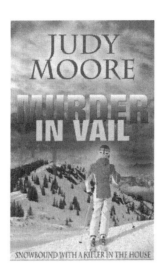

Sally Braddock's serene lifestyle atop a mountain in Vail, Colorado, changes drastically each year when her three spoiled children and their spouses visit her – and her money – for Christmas. They live off their trust funds, which are disappearing quickly, and spend most of the holidays bickering and hitting up their mother for money.

This year, Sally makes an announcement that sends her children into a tizzy, an announcement so extreme that it pushes someone in the house to murder. The storm inside the house is matched by a raging blizzard outside, and the family finds themselves snowbound with a killer.

Judy Moore

354

Excerpt from Murder in Vail

Chapter One

It was Christmas, so Sally had to see her children. And worse, their dreadful spouses.

Her three children visited her—and her money— only once a year, and a few days each year were plenty. Sally could barely tolerate them anymore. None of them worked, had children, helped charities, or knew how to do much of anything except spend money. They lived off their trust funds, and those funds were disappearing quickly.

Sally really couldn't figure out where she went wrong. She'd read every parenting book available back in the eighties, and she stayed at home to raise her kids. But her children had grown into the most materialistic, useless adults she'd ever met. And their spouses were even worse.

It must have been the money, she told herself. All that money.

Her husband's family had millions, which he had turned into billions. When he died of a heart attack at age fifty-one, Sally became one of the first female billionaires in North America. She often wondered what her life would have been like if she hadn't met Jack Braddock at the Pan American Games when they were both twenty-one. She was just a suntanned, middle-class girl from Southern California. But she competed on the U.S. synchronized swimming team, and he rode for the Canadian cycling squad. She medaled. He didn't.

The attraction between them had been immediate, and they became inseparable from the day they met. She had no idea he came from one of the wealthiest steel families in Canada. They married six months later. She accompanied him to the Olympic Games the next year—where he finished in the middle of the pack—but she couldn't compete because synchronized swimming had yet to become an Olympic sport. By the time it was, she had two children and another one on the way.

Sally and her husband had been so happy together for thirty years. Then he died, and she was suddenly alone. That was nearly six years ago, and since she'd lived by herself with her two Labradoodles and her housekeeper on top of a mountain near Vail, Colorado. It had been their second home since the children were young, and Sally moved in full-time after Jack died. Living in Canada for most of their married life, Sally and Jack loved winter sports and took up skiing together. With their athletic ability, they became so proficient that helicopter skiing held the only challenge for them. They skied down mountains in Colorado other skiers didn't even know existed.

The biggest disappointment of her husband's life was that none of his children took any interest in the family steel business. Now it was run by a board of directors made up of outsiders. Still the primary shareholder, Sally's only participation was to attend the annual meeting every year in Toronto.

Her husband had set up trust funds for their three children in hopes they would build businesses of their own. They received twenty-five million dollars each when they turned twenty-four years old. Her husband chose the age and the amount—that was how much his family's business was worth when he took it over when he was twenty-four. By the time he died, his personal fortune had grown to more than three billion dollars. But the opposite was the case with her children. Each year, their fortunes became more and more depleted.

In retrospect, Sally wished they had paid more attention to the advice of another billionaire, Warren Buffett. His philosophy? "Give your children enough to do anything, but not enough to do nothing." Great advice. Sally and her husband had given their children enough to do nothing—and that is exactly what they had done. It had been a huge mistake giving them that much money at such a young age, a decision Sally would always regret. The money her children already had received was the last they would get from her. Sally was adamant about that. She planned to follow Buffett's example this time and give the vast majority of her fortune to charity.

At fifty-six, Sally stayed active supporting several charities, painting watercolors, skiing, and of course, swimming. She swam for an hour every day in her large outdoor pool, summer or winter, many times when it was snowing. Sometimes she even practiced her old synchronized swimming routines. As a result, she had the body of a forty-year-old.

It was snowing today, two days before Christmas, as she backstroked across the long, infinity pool. She could see the snow-capped peaks of the Rocky Mountains in the distance, rising behind the steam that floated off the heated swimming pool. The snowflakes felt so cool as they fluttered down onto her face, refreshing her in these final minutes of her hour-long swim.

A few more circles of angels and that will be it for today, she thought, scissor-kicking out to the center of the pool. She floated for a few moments, then brought her right foot up to her left knee and lifted it straight into the air, pointing her toes. Sculling evenly with her hands underwater, she moved in a large circle around the middle of the pool for several seconds, her extended leg perfectly straight. She could have gone longer, but the twenty-eight degree temperature became too uncomfortable for the exposed leg.

Finally, she swam to the shallow end, stepped out of the pool, and picked up one of the thick beach towels that were stacked by the pool's edge. Shaking the snow from the towel, Sally quickly dried off and tied it around her waist. She grabbed a second towel and flung it around her shoulders, pulling it snugly around the top of her one-piece white bathing suit. The icy wind slapped at her bare skin as she hurried across the two-tiered deck, past the hot tub, to the back door of the house.

She stepped into the warmth of the kitchen and scurried over to the small fire that was ablaze under the brick hearth. As she warmed her hands at the fire, she could feel the endorphin rush begin to engulf her body, bringing that familiar feeling of peace and tranquility.

Then the doorbell rang.

Made in the USA
Columbia, SC
16 October 2017